LAST ONE ALIVE

Kristopher Rufty

This book is a work of fiction. The names, characters, places, and incidents are products of the writer's imagination or have been used fictitiously and are not to be construed as real. Any resemblance to persons living or dead, actual events, locale or organizations is entirely coincidental.

Last One Alive
Text Copyright © 2013 by Kristopher Rufty
Second Paperback Edition
Copyright © 2021 by Kristopher Rufty
Cover art copyright © 2021

All Rights Are Reserved. No part of this book may be used or reproduced in any manner whatsoever without written permission, except in the case of brief quotations embodied in critical articles and reviews.

ISBN: 9798504457345

LAZARUS PRESS

DEDICATION

For Vanelle.

1

A scream snapped Megan's eyes open.
Her head on the pillow, she listened, hearing nothing but the chorales of crickets and frogs outside her tent.

The fog in her head began to dispel, clearing just enough for her to comprehend very little.

Had she heard a scream?

She listened even harder but heard nothing else.

Just as she was about to chalk it off as a bad dream, squeals from outside stopped her breath.

That sounded like Allison.

Slowly, she sat up. She pressed her fists to her eyes and rubbed the sleep out. The sleeping bag dropped away from her chest, exposing her breasts to the mild, early morning mountain air. Her nipples stiffened against the chill. She felt her skin pebbling up with goose bumps.

Megan had opted to snooze in the sack the same as she did at home: in nothing but panties. Being alone in her tent, she hadn't bothered with extra clothing. It had been warm zipped tightly in the sack, but without it, freezing. Hard to believe it was late June. During the daylight, hiking the trails, she'd yearned for a break from the heat, but now she yearned for the heat. And that was the extent of her love-hate relationship with Mother Nature.

Feeling around the tent, her fingers found a smooth piece of fabric. Felt like her tank top. She held it up. It was. She quickly threw it over her head and tugged it down. It did little to warm her, but at least her breasts were covered.

Faint moaning from outside. Zero pleasure in its tenor.

What are they doing?

Megan turned around, found her carry bag, and opened it. She shuffled through the inside, retrieving a flashlight. It was a small plastic tube that ran on two AA batteries. She clicked it on to make sure it worked. It did. She quickly cut it back off.

Then she dropped down on her rump and began to seek out her shorts.

She quickly found them under her backpack. She pulled them up her legs and over her rump, then located her new hiking shoes. She'd bought them last weekend in preparation for this four-day excursion.

Her socks were poking out the tops like pale wool

flowers in a pot. She pulled the socks halfway up her shins, then slid them back down to where they bunched around her ankle. The boots still felt a little tight as she laced them, even after the six miles of hiking today. She'd expected the leather to have been broken in by now. Another day like they had today should do it.

Megan crawled to the flap at the front. She unzipped it. Poking out her head from behind the flap, she looked from left to right. All seemed to be in order—desolate and dark, but in order.

She looked up. The sky was no longer an inundating lake of oil around the island of the moon with stars floating amid the obscurity like little bubbles. Veins of purple were beginning to seep through, trumpeting the oncoming sunrise. Not much more than an hour and the sun should have taken its position for the start of another hot, sticky day.

Another day without Matt.

She quickly stopped thinking about him before he brought her even more tears. She'd cried because of him enough already. Plus, she'd promised Allison she wouldn't allow herself to miss him during their trip. But that had been almost impossible. Whenever she saw Allison and Brian lovingly snuggling up on each other, trading smooches, it reminded her of his absence, especially since he was originally supposed to have been on this trip.

Plans change when you find out they've been fucking someone else.

Stop thinking about it!

Megan crawled out of the tent. The chilly air covered her like a blanket soaked in ice. She stood up, stretching her back and legs. Her calves were sore and achy, her thighs tight and painful.

She hadn't been to the mountains since last summer. And that had been with Matt, of course. Not even a full year, but judging how her legs were feeling, it could have been three. She'd also put on a little weight, not much, but she was noticeably thicker. Allison and Brian denied she'd gotten heavier. But remembering how her old hiking shorts could no longer button in the front was all the proof she really needed.

And this was only the start of the second day. Still one more left after this one of going up and down hills, rocky ridges, and very steep inclines.

I'm toast.

At least all the strenuous activities should help her shed some pounds, and the dehydrated cuisine they were ingesting would also help.

Even with the sun beginning its ascent, it was still dark around their campsite, even darker still in the areas outside their camp where the trees were thicker.

Megan clicked on the flashlight. The weak beam raked over the extinguished campfire, then raised and settled onto the other tent.

Keeping her voice down, she said "Allison? Brian?"

She stopped in front of the neighboring tent. A sly smiled arched her lips. A new idea began to manifest.

Maybe she'd misunderstood the cries and moans. What if she was wrong thinking they were pain-filled? Allison and Brian could be partaking in some abusive lovemaking, mixing a little pain with pleasure.

Making it hurt so good?

Very possible.

But this early in the morning?

She thought so. Most likely, they'd started fooling around while getting ready to cook breakfast—it was their turn—and it had escalated from there. A morning quickie.

Then again, what if they weren't?

But what else could it be?

If they were being hurt...

No. No one's hurting them.

Still...

"Guys," she called, louder this time. "Are you doing something I shouldn't see?" She waited, then tried again, teasingly. "Allisooooon? Briaaaaaan?"

Nothing still.

If this was a prank, they were really dragging it out. She might want to check their tent, then again, she might not. What would she see if she looked inside? Two bare asses gaping back at her?

Megan squatted by the front flap. "Last chance to let me know you're in there screwing around, or just *screwing*. I'm coming in, and I might see you in your bare necessities." She waited a beat. "All right. You had your chance."

Unzipping the flap with one hand, she kept the light

held up by her face and aimed forward with the other.

Megan expected the musky scent of sex to waft out from the tent. It did not. Instead, she was met with an odd combination of copper and beef, like the odor whenever she tore the cellophane away from a pack of raw steaks.

Opening her eyes, they continued to stretch wide until she could feel them tugging at the thin skin near her sockets. She opened her mouth to scream, but her lips could only tremble around the sharp gasps of air huffing out. Her chest bounced up and down with each pant.

Inside the tent was Brian's torso—or what was left of it.

2

The head, arms, and legs were absent, leaving behind only ragged stumps, stems, and sinewy ligaments.

Megan loosed a scream as she stammered backwards. She landed hard on her rump, machine-gunning shrieks as she scrambled away from the tent. She managed to hold on to the flashlight, although her arm was wailing and flinging itself this way and that.

A dry crunching noise, something like a footstep, resounded from the woods. She whipped around, jabbing the flashlight in the direction of the noise. She saw nothing. Her legs felt like boiled noodles. She wanted them to cooperate with her, to stiffen so she could stand, but they remained limp and soggy.

Megan's mind reeled over the image she'd just seen: Brian's torso, lack of appendages and head. She knew it was Brian's by his *Game Over* shirt. He'd bought it in New Orleans the same night he'd proposed to Allison.

Allison!

Without thinking, she shined the light back into the tent. She did her best to avoid seeing the grotesque remains of Brian. It was impossible though. He was spread out all over the place.

Blood had painted the tent's interior, dripping from the ceiling in tiny red droplets. Jagged strips of flesh and sinewy chunks of meat were strewn across the blankets and sleeping bags. All of it seemed to match the devastated body of Brian.

Allison was not in there.

Relief washed over Megan. It was brief, however, when she realized she didn't know where Allison was.

If she wasn't in the tent…

Did she *do this to Brian?*

That idea survived a matter of two seconds before being shot down. There was no way in hell. It wasn't that Megan found Allison incapable of hurting someone. Just not Brian, ever. They were a couple most believed God had specifically created to share their lives together. No longer just Brian or just Allison, but a partnership, combined personalities, two separate beings that had stopped existing on their own merits and began to exist for each other.

She'd often referred to them as *Brianison.*

So if Allison wasn't in the tent, then where was she?

Yet another cry resounded from the woods. Female.

Its pitiful tone crushed Megan. She listened, heard it again, fainter.

"Allison," she gasped.

The whimper had come from the woods. Megan stood. Her legs wobbled under her, threatening to fold, but thankfully did not. She took a few steadying breaths, then bobbled toward the patch of trees. Allison was out there, she was certain.

Hunched over like someone holding in a pee, the flashlight pointing ahead of her stabbing washed-out light through the dark, she put a shaky finger to her lips and chewed at the tip. A nervous habit she'd had since she was little, and even now she didn't realize she was doing it.

Megan entered the woods. She stepped around the frontline of trees. It was much darker on this side of their campsite. The trees were taller, thicker. Diffused moonlight was netted through heavy, leaf-filled branches. The flashlight landed on clots in the dirt. Something wet had splashed on the trail, coagulating the dirt into mud. She squatted down for a closer look. The ground was darker in color here, thicker in texture, but she couldn't tell if it was because of the soil or whatever had been spilled on it. She followed a dotted trail to some heavier dabs on the brush beside her. On the leaves it was much easier to tell the darkness was actually made by the liquid itself.

And it wasn't just *any* liquid.

It was blood.

A lot of it.

Her throat made a strangled whine. Her finger returned to her mouth, where she gnawed at it so hard it hurt. She quickly pulled the finger away from her teeth. She'd broken the skin.

Megan gave another quick scan of the blood spatters, then leaped to her feet.

"Allison!" Her voice was raspy and shrill.

She walked alongside the thicket of trees. Reaching the end of this patch, she turned left.

"Alli—?" The name stopped short on her tongue. She stopped walking. Her eyes bulged at what she saw.

In front of her, Allison was on all fours, her weight shifted to one side with lacerations lining her back under the blood sousing her pajamas. It was hard to decipher the severity of her wounds, but they must have been pretty bad from how deep her shirt sank into her back.

At least she was alive.

Megan rushed to her, dropped to her knees, and slid to a halt. Ignoring the burning on her knees, she reached out to her friend. Her hands stopped just shy of touching Allison. She was quenched in a *lot* of blood. How much of it was hers and how much was Brian's was hard to tell. She grimaced at the copious amount. It seemed Allison was drowning in it.

And Megan was *not* the squeamish type. She'd seen this much blood before, even worse, while on duty in the ER, but seeing it on her friend—someone she considered her sister—put it on a different level entirely.

She was also afraid of adding even more pain to Allison by touching her.

"Al? It's me."

"Muh-Megan?" she said without looking up. Her head hung low enough to the ground that her nose was probably brushing coarse bits of dirt. Her hair was much shorter than Megan's, especially in the back, but Allison kept her bangs shaggy. Now they were sweat-soaked and plastered across her forehead. "Is it…you?"

"It's me, Al. It's me." Her throat tightened. Allison began to go blurry in her eyes from the tears suddenly flooding them.

"I woke up…heard someone at the tent. I thought it was Brian, you know…playing around or something. We'd been fighting earlier…and Brian stormed out of the tent. I went to sleep…"

"Allison…" She tried to stop her from talking, but Allison kept going as if she had a speed button on her mouth set to high.

"…so I opened the tent and the moonlight came in, lighting up the inside, you know?" Allison groaned as she straightened her shoulders. She looked at Megan, now, as she talked. There were bruises on her face, dirt adhered to her face in dark streaks. "I happened to look back…at Brian's sleeping bag and guess what I saw."

"Al, we should get—"

"—Guess!"

Megan flinched at the sudden rise in her voice. Her friend's eyes looked like white orbs on a face smudged in dirt, scabbing abrasions, and dried blood. "I don't…I have no idea!"

"Brian was sleeping in the sack!" She laughed. There seemed to be no good sense left in her. "By then it was too late. He came into the tent, killed Brian like *that!*" She snapped her finger, but it made no sound. "Then he punched me on the head, hard. I woke up as he was dragging me out, but I couldn't move. It was like I was paralyzed or some shit."

Megan winced from the pain when she bit back down on the finger she'd previously wounded with her teeth.

Allison hadn't let up. "I tried to shout for you, to warn you, but I couldn't. I thought you might already be dead…"

"I was sleeping. Goddammit, I was sleeping. I'm so sorry…"

"There's no way you could have heard him, he moved so fast and was so *quiet.*" Her eyes widened even more, so much so the skin around them might split apart. "I thought he was a *ghost.*"

A ghost…

A chill moved through Megan so deep that she felt it in the marrow of her bones.

"He began attacking me with this…sword or something."

"A sword?"

"No, not really a sword, but it could have been. It—a *big* fucking knife! So fucking big! Like the ones you see in the movies! He just kept hitting me with it and hitting me with me it. Not too hard, but hard *enough.*" She took several rapid breaths before continuing. "I pretended to be dead. But I don't know if he, you know, believed it."

"He left, so he must have."

"I…don't know. I don't think he fell for it."

"What'd he look like?"

Allison stared up as if a picture of him might be projected across the sky. Megan could see her much clearer now. She realized the sun had risen even more and was now spreading its warm, golden shower across the woods. The temperature would begin its swift ascend over the next couple hours. "Big," she finally answered. "He's still out here…somewhere. I don't know where!" Her head snapped back and forth as she searched the grounds for him.

"He's probably at the camp going …" Megan didn't complete the statement. But if she had it would have sounded like this: *Probably at the camp, going after me.*

She took Allison's hands in hers. They felt sticky and cold. "We have to get you on your feet. Can you stand up?"

Allison thought about it. "Yuh-yeah…probably. If you help me."

"I will. Do you think you can find the way back to your car?"

"I-I don't know…Brian…he was the one with the map…"

"Can *you* remember?"

Megan hoped Allison could, because her own

memory of how they got down here was fuzzy. This was her first time in this area, and she was out of practice. So instead of noting her surroundings, or any interesting landmarks, she'd only cussed to herself at how miserable she was—and also hating herself for falling out of shape so quickly.

It was up to Allison to get them back. Going back to the camp was out of the question. Megan would have bet all she owned that whoever had attacked Allison and killed Brian was there right now.

Might even be on his way back. Surely he's noticed I'm not in my tent.

"Can you?" Megan snapped at Allison.

"Yuh-yeah, I should be able to. It wasn't such a hard hike…pretty simple."

My ass.

Allison added, "I probably can get us to the car…"

"Let's try."

Megan ignored her apprehension of touching her critically injured friend and helped her get on her feet.

3

The sun was up, the heat thicker and more intense. Although the breezes were scarce, Megan was thankful for each one that came. She'd tucked the flashlight into the elastic band of her shorts. It rubbed against her sweaty skin, making a patch at her hip tender and raw. She poked out her bottom lip and puffed a blast of air into her soaked bangs. Sprigs of hair shot back with the rest. Her eyes burned as sweat dribbled into them. She could taste the salty warmth on her upper lip.

Megan doubted they'd traveled much distance. It felt as if they were moving slower than time. She wouldn't be surprised if they hadn't gone a mile yet.

With an arm around Allison's back, Megan held her up, and had been virtually dragging her most of the way. Allison was hurt, yes, but she hadn't been putting in any effort to move about on her own. In fact, she constantly made the trek even more complicated by looking behind them every few feet.

Allison did it again, this time almost making both of them fall.

"Stop looking back!" Megan demanded.

"I can't help it—he's coming after us, I just *know* it!"

"Then that's why you should move *faster*, dammit! That way he *can't* catch us."

"Yeah. Right. Okay." Allison was fading away in her mind. Her eyes gave it away with their wide and shocked, yet blankly abandoned gaze. "Okay." But she didn't move any faster. She seemed to decrease in speed even more.

Megan was growing furious with her friend. The temptation to leave her behind while she went and located the car on her own was there, but she chose not to acknowledge it.

"Do you think you can walk on your own?" she asked Allison. "We can move faster."

They stopped walking. Allison looked hesitant, frightened of trying. "I-I don't know."

"We're not making any progress doing it this way."

"I...I probably can do it."

"Let's try." Megan gently pulled out of Allison's constrictive grip. Her friend's blood was stained across her hip and thigh. Her clothes clung to her from the blood and her own sweat.

Taking a couple steps, Allison continued stealing

glances over her shoulder.

"He's not back there," said Megan. "Not yet." She was starting to wonder if there really was someone back there.

Of course there is. Look at Allison. That's your proof.

What if Brian did that to her?

Oh sure, and then went back and cut off his head, legs, and arms to cover up. Sure.

"I think I can make it," said Allison. "But I'll have to move slow..."

"Any speed you go on your own will be faster than what we've been doing together."

"Yeah..." Allison looked regretful, as if this was her fault. "Sorry."

"Don't be. Let's just keep moving."

"Okay..."

"You lead. I'll follow."

Megan trailed a couple of feet behind Allison for what felt like hours, but she figured it was actually closer to only one. She tried keeping her eyes ahead of her, and her ears focused on everything else. It didn't work. She found herself being too distracted by Allison's wounds, and the excruciatingly slow momentum of her steps.

At least some of the gashes looked to have stopped bleeding. The stains on her skin were becoming flaky and brown, no longer moist and red. But the blood was also attracting flies and mosquitoes, even ants. This probably added to Allison's speed, which added to

Megan's aggravation.

I could just have her sit down by a tree or something. She could tell me how to get back to the car.

Then what? Just drive it through the woods to come and get Allison? Knock down trees with the front bumper? Sure. That would work just fine.

Whatever. Think with your brain, idiot.

She couldn't rightfully leave Allison behind.

Megan continued to walk as Allison staggered ahead of her. A hint of animal dung hovered in the air. Something had gone number two nearby. She hoped it was a deer and not anything bigger than that. Birds seemed to be competing with one another for the loudest chirp in various tenors and bars.

Megan watched Allison drag her bare feet across the ground, scraping her toes across jutting roots and acorns that were sprinkled all over. She cringed each time a toenail caught on something, making her stumble. She wished Allison had on shoes. It would protect her feet and might speed things up.

I could probably give her mine. I could still move faster barefoot than she is.

She was about to suggest it to Allison when she spotted a bush over to her left. A bush that looked very familiar. *Too* familiar. "Hold up."

"Huh?"

"Stop walking."

"Gladly…" Ceasing her travels, she turned around to face Megan. "Taking a break?"

Megan ignored the question as she approached the bush. She saw the leaves, then checked the ground around it to be sure. She knew exactly where they were. And dammit…this was not where they needed to be. "We've been here already."

"Wha…?" Allison jerked rigid, then winced. "What do you mean?"

"Right over here is where I found you!" She pointed to her left where Allison's blood was interspersed about the forestry in an assortment of consistencies. "Just look!"

Allison tottered closer. When she saw what Megan was pointing at, a sobbing breakdown threatened to get away from her.

Megan continued. "If this is the spot where I found you, then that means the tents are right over there!" This time, she pointed straight ahead of them. "Right where we're fucking going!"

"How did this happen?"

"How the hell should I know!? But somehow we walked in one big fucking circle!" She pushed Allison, causing her to stumble backwards. Luckily, she didn't fall, or Megan would have felt even worse than she did the moment her hands touched Allison's chest.

The betrayed, heartbroken expression on Allison's face was like a knife to Megan's heart.

"I'm sorry, Allison…" She shook her head in disbelief at herself. "I shouldn't have done that…" Tears of frustration, defeat, and shame were welling up in her eyes. "Sorry…"

If Allison had heard the apology, she gave zero indication. "What are we going to do now!?" Her breaths sounded like something sharp swiping across glass. "I'm hurting all over…and I'm dizzy…I can't keep walking…"

"This was your doing. You led us right back here!"

"I tried, okay! I tried to get us back to the car! I just got turned around!"

"You fucked up is what you did!"

"Well, forgive me for letting being attacked with a sword and witnessing my soon-to-be-husband getting butchered mess up my sense of direction. Fuck me sideways! Guess I shouldn't let petty shit like that mess with my sense of direction!"

Now, Megan felt *really* lousy.

Way to go, bitch.

Megan sighed. "I'm sorry…I'm not meaning to take this out on you—"

"—well you are!"

Megan closed her eyes, taking a deep breath before talking. "You're right, and I'm sorry. But since we're at our tents, let's use it to our advantage, all right?"

"How?"

"I'll grab some water, and I have a first-aid kit in my tent that I can use to patch you up some. It's not much, but it's better than nothing."

"Yeah…"

"We need to get you some socks and shoes, too."

"They're in the tent…with…"

"*I'll* get them."

Allison looked relieved. "Thank you."

"And we need to do it quickly. I have a bad feeling…"

4

The campsite looked peacefully convivial. It was hard to believe that any kind of grisly events had taken place here only a short time ago. There was a heavy sheaf of shade over the camp that made it feel ten degrees cooler. Nature was going about her day as if nothing had happened.

Megan wanted nothing more than to crawl in her tent and lie down for a few hours. She was exhausted already and still had many miles to hike back to the car with an injured person that she assumed she would be carrying before long. That would, at the very least, double the time it would take to get back to the car—if they could even find it.

Don't think like that. You can do this. You have to. There's no choice.

Megan looked at Allison's tent. On the other side of

those nylon walls was the gory aftermath of a massacre. She felt tight and sick inside. All her insecurities rushed over her as if they'd been dumped from a bucket over her head.

Allison staggered out of the woods. Her eyes immediately locked on the tent as well. "You can see where he dragged me…"

Megan followed Allison's gaze and spotted a path on the ground where the grass had been mashed down. It was easy to overlook in the dark, but now she couldn't miss it. She pictured Allison, dazed, being dragged along the ground by her feet, the tents and campsite becoming smaller the farther away she got.

"Oh, Brian…" Allison began to sob, her shoulders bouncing heavily by her head. "*Briiiiiaaaannn!*" Tears streamed from her eyes as her mouth trembled violently. She looked so pitiful.

Megan hurried to Allison and pulled her tightly against her. She stroked Allison's back. It felt gluey and hot under her hand. "Calm down…calm down."

"I c-c-can't calm down." She choked on a whine. As she tried to breathe, her bottom lip sniffled over her teeth. She sounded like a little girl. "Brian's dead. He's *dead*!"

"Allison, you have to calm down, and I'm sorry to say this—*shut* your damn mouth. Whoever attacked you is probably out there looking for us. I'm sure he knows that you're alive and he also probably put two and two together that the empty tent over there with the all-girl stuff inside is missing its sleeper."

"I *can't!*"

Megan pushed Allison back and quickly slapped her cheek.

Allison's cries stopped at once. Shock replaced the sadness. She slowly raised a hand to her cheek. "Ow…"

"I'm sorry…"

"You slapped me, you *bitch*!"

"I had to make you stop!"

"You didn't have to *slap* me!"

"We need to get what we came for and get moving. We're wasting too much time."

Allison nodded against her hand. "Yuh-yeah, yuh-you're right."

"I'm going to get some water out of my tent and my first-aid kit. I'll patch you up the best I can, then I'll get your shoes on your feet, and we can *go*."

"Okay."

"Sit down where we roasted marshmallows last night."

Megan watched Allison take a seat on one of the logs positioned in front the charred-black pyramid of sticks. She remembered how much fun they'd had last night, and how delicious the marshmallows had tasted after being scorched. Not once had Matt crossed her mind.

And he was now? Seriously?

"Hurry up," said Allison, calling her back from the memory.

Sounded as if Allison was regaining her wits, and this was good. Megan was glad to have her back. "Two shakes," said Megan, darting toward her tent. As she was about to enter, she paused.

Squatting, her hand hovered in front of the flap. Then she remembered she hadn't closed the tent when she'd clambered out of it. She'd left the flap dangling.

What if he's in there waiting for me?

"What's wrong?" Allison called from behind her.

Too late to try for the element of surprise.

"Nuh-nothing," answered Megan, shaking her head. If he was in there, he surely knew she was right outside. Either way, she couldn't get the jump on him.

She still needed to at least check. Maybe he'd searched inside, then sealed it back up when he was done.

Why would he do that?

So she'd know he'd been here.

Megan's skin went tight and crawly. Somehow, she knew that was exactly what he'd done.

Here goes.

Pinching the zipper between her forefinger and thumb, she ran it along the teeth. Before the flap could drop, she pushed it in, ready to leap back and run if she had to.

There was no need. The tent was empty.

Megan rushed inside.

Her cooler-pack was at the back of the tent. She opened it, removed two bottles of water, and set one of them down. She twisted off the cap of the one she kept, chugging until the bottle was empty. Discarding it over her shoulder, she took another from the cooler.

It took longer to locate the first-aid kit than she

would have liked. Opening the lid, she rummaged through its contents, sighing when all she could find was some band-aids, two patch-bandages, and disinfectant spray.

"It'll have to do," she muttered, closing the lid.

Then she grabbed her backpack, dumped out the useless crap, and tossed in some water, the kit, and a blanket. She pulled the flashlight out from her shorts, dropping it into the backpack as well.

Looking around the tent one last time, she decided she had everything she needed.

Megan zipped her pack and scooted up to the exit. She pulled the flap back, ready to depart, but promptly stopped. Her hand rose to her mouth, trembling fingers cupping her lips.

Oh. My. God.

Allison sat on the log, rubbing her arms that were probably throbbing, and staring absently at the ground. Megan had expected that. But what she hadn't counted on was the large man standing behind her.

He was garbed in bedraggled clothing—long pants, boots, a long-sleeved shirt rolled up to the elbows. He must have been seven feet tall with straps crisscrossed over his chest, each one attaching a separate, two-bladed ax to his back like swords. A knife was sheathed around the thigh of his left leg.

And the final piece of his attire was a mask—crudely made, perceptibly by his own hands. It looked trussed over the bushel of unkempt hair that sprouted from his head in wild frizzes. The mask was crafted of a thick, leathery materiel—sections had been sewed and *patched up* with other types of materials—and covered his face, dangling down to the top of his chest in a ragged point. Serrated slits had been made for the eyes.

He was filthy, his skin smudged with dark spots, and even from her tent, Megan could see how his blackened fingernails were long and jagged like broken talons. He looked as if he'd survived in the wilderness for quite some time.

The *sword* Allison had declared was actually a machete, but the biggest that Megan had ever seen. Clutched in his right hand, the gargantuan blade dangled by his leg.

A walking monstrosity.

And Allison was oblivious to his presence.

5

"Allison."

Megan had hoped to get her attention with a shouting whisper, but no sound had been made when she mouthed her friend's name. She tried again.

"Allison." A bit louder this time, but still not loud enough.

Allison continued sitting on the log, staring at either the ground or her feet while rubbing the back of her neck. Megan reached for the flap, then hesitated. She *wanted* to pull Allison away from the monstrous maniac but was so frightened that she couldn't move.

Allison raised her head, rolling it around on her shoulders. A staccato chain of pops and cracks followed. She sighed. Her eyes locked on Megan hunkering down in the tent. Her face scrunched up with confusion. She opened her mouth to say something, but Megan quickly waved her arms, hoping she would understand that she was telling her not to speak.

"What!" called Allison, loudly.

Megan's heart lurched in her chest.

My God, doesn't she understand anything?

She continued to wave her hands, pointing over Allison's shoulder, trying to warn her that someone was behind her. She even began mouthing: *Get away from there.*

Allison didn't seem to grasp it. "What's wrong with you?"

Megan slapped a finger to her lips, silently shushing Allison. She stopped talking. At least that had worked. Allison looked even more confused, watching Megan miming with her hands—pointing past her shoulder, then using her thumb to point another direction.

Whether Allison understood the warnings or not, she was beginning to realize something was wrong. Allison sniffed a few times, grimacing at the odor her nose must have caught. Though Megan couldn't *actually* smell the maniac, she guessed his smell was less than pleasant.

Megan mimed the motions one more time.

It clicked.

Allison swallowed. Hard. Instead of fleeing, she slowly looked back over her shoulder. Her entire body began to tremble.

She sees him. God oh God, she sees him. Please

Allison, run. RUN!

Standing massively like a statue placed there, and all Allison seemed to know how to do was shiver and quake.

His free hand lashed out and gripped onto the back of Allison's neck. He raised her off the ground like a kitten, then dropped the machete where it imbedded itself, blade down, into the ground.

Allison's feet dangled limply as if his grip paralyzed her. Her pleading eyes found Megan, and she could feel her friend begging to be rescued. But as horrible as it made her feel—like a coward, chicken shit—Megan knew she wouldn't be leaving the tent. Her legs felt weighted down with lead. She could only watch with a hand cupped over her mouth.

The maniac squeezed Allison's neck. Then, using his other hand, he grabbed her chin and wrenched her head around in one quick motion. A loud succession of splintering cracks resounded through the still air. Allison went limp. When the man was done, Allison's face was positioned above her spine. A mound of lumpy, dough-like flesh was amassed at the side of her neck. Megan could see the front of her body and the back of her head at the same time.

He released her. Allison dropped to the ground in a lifeless thud.

The maniac towered over Allison, gazing down at his work completed. Time seemed to stand still. Megan could hear nothing but the rumbling whoosh of blood pumping deep in her ears. Her breathing felt as if it had slowed to an infrequent puff.

It was like existing inside a photograph. Nothing moved. Nothing seemed real, only fabricated, and enhanced by the photographer's lens.

Everything kicked back to normal when he whipped his head around and looked directly at Megan. She jumped back as if she'd been shoved. He tilted his head to one side, then raised it up straight. Leaning over, his grimy fingers curled around the machete's hilt, and he tugged it from the ground.

Oh God!

He took a step toward her.

6

Megan quickly zipped the flap shut. It would do nothing to keep him out, but it might slow him down, not by much, but possibly some.

She hated herself for many things during this moment. One of them was allowing her friend to die while she'd watched.

What could I do, really?

There was *nothing* she could have done, and that was another reason why she hated herself. She had no weapon unless she counted her fists. But with only her hands going against a monster that could twist a person's head around like they were twisting the cap off a bottle, there was no way she could have been a threat.

Still, she wasn't just going to lie back and let him do his worse to her. She was going to fight to live. But how she intended on doing that, she had no clue.

Megan scooted to the middle of the tent. She looked around, trying to find something she could use for a weapon. She remembered Brian had a hunter's knife, but assumed it was in the other tent with what remained of him. Again, she hated herself for not bringing anything of her own.

The man's frame blocked the sun, a heavy darkness encroaching the tent. Megan jerked her head towards the front. He was right outside. Before she could absorb the fact that he was within a couple of feet of her, the *machete* ripped through the front of the tent.

Screaming, she crab-crawled to the back.

The blade pierced down from the ceiling, missing her by a few inches. She hadn't even noticed he'd torn it out from the front side. He could easily just rip the tent open with his hands, or the simpler way, unzip the front and crawl in, but he did neither. He was going after her this way, Megan figured, to play with her some before the actual killing, like a cat having fun with a mouse before the fatal bite.

Rolling onto her stomach, Megan kept as low as she could. The blade plunged even farther down, stopping right in front of her face. She looked at the blade and could smell the tarnished metal as it twisted and was yanked back out.

Megan sat up. She looked every which way.

I'm trapped.

Everything around her was chaotic. Looking up front, she saw his outline circling back around to the main flap. He reached through the slit made by his machete, using his hands to tear it wider.

An idea sparked. Megan looked at the slit in the rear of the tent. If he was trying to tear his way through the front, then she would do the same in the back. On all fours, she crawled to the back wall. Her knees pummeled the ground. By the time she reached the other slit, her knees had almost stopped working.

With both hands, she began tugging at the slash. It spread easily enough. She stole a glance over her shoulder and saw the hole she'd left behind was wide enough that he raised a muck-covered boot into the gap and stepped down—ripping the tent all the way to the ground.

Megan screamed. He was a lot closer to getting in than she was to getting out.

No longer caring how big the hole was, she decided to make a go for it. Her head and shoulders sprung through, but her breasts clogged her. Pushing harder, she forced them through, but her hips snagged her next. She squelched a whimper.

Wriggling, she shimmied her hips in hopes of dislodging them. The tent was starting to give. She pawed at the ground, gripping handfuls of grass, and thrusting with all she had. Her hips nudged through a little more. She was nearly free. One more heave should do it.

Then she felt a warm, calloused hand grip her ankle.

Felt herself being pulled back in without any effort. She struggled against him, and to her surprise broke free.

Before he could grab her again, she kicked at him.

Nothing connected.

Another grip on her ankle. "Let go of me!" she shrilled.

He did not release her, but he also wasn't trying to pull her back in. As she began to question why, a stinging sensation lit up her calf in a straight line.

He's cutting me!

She squirmed, kicking her feet up and down as if throwing a tantrum. Finally, she tore away from his grasp, pulled her feet out, and crashed on the ground. As much as it hurt, she didn't allow it to deter her escape. She rolled away from the tent, and gave her calf a quick glance, dabbing up the trickling blood with a finger. The incision was too thin and small to have been made by his machete. She remembered the knife sheathed to his leg. One that size could cause a wound like this.

Wincing, Megan rose to her feet. She did a quick look around, trying to determine the best way to go.

The machete ripped through the top of the tent, followed by hands tearing the material. Screaming once again, she just ran in no particular direction, only caring that it was *away* from him.

As the man ripped his way out of the tent, survival was all that concerned her now.

7

Amanda Carpenter used a pencil to poke around a small, discarded bag of trash on the dirt road. Judging the contents inside, she doubted it had belonged to those she was looking for.

She dropped the pencil in the bag with the rest of the litter. She wasn't going to use the pencil again knowing it had been prodding around someone's trash. Then she stood up, brushing off her hands on the seat of her shorts. Dusty fingerprints were now speckled across the khaki-colored fabric.

She was glad she'd worn shorts today. It was barely ten, and already hot as hell. Because she was alone out here, she'd left her uniform shirt unbuttoned. What breeze there was felt wonderful against the square of chest not covered by the white tank top underneath her Elk Grove Forest Ranger's shirt. The tops of her breasts were slick with sweat, and the hollow of her throat poured even more perspiration down the valley between their slopes. If she was to come across any hikers, she'd be sure to button up, but for now she was just going to leave it open to the air. She might even shed the tan-colored heat trapper altogether.

Amanda had left her Jeep parked in a turnoff several feet back. With the bag of trash in tote, she made her way back to her ride. Her boots crunched gravel as she walked the short stride to the Jeep.

Stopping by the taillight, she turned away, facing the way she'd come from. She gazed upon the dense forestry ahead of her, beside her, and behind her.

Where are you, you bastards?

The peaceful serenity of Mother Nature hung all around her. Countless species of birds cheeped from every direction. A mild breeze drifted over, carrying with it the sweet smell of pine and wood. It was lovely, but also very deceiving. Such a gorgeous shell that once it was cracked open unveiled horrors hidden inside: shiners, poachers, dangerously wild animals, and more, so much more.

"Amanda?"

Amanda yelped when a distorted voice slashed through the stillness.

"Amanda? Come in."

Her heart rattled against her chest. Glancing over her shoulder, she looked at the Jeep, its windows down.

Paul.

Trying not to smile, she moseyed around the front and crawled into the driver seat. Her CB radio was mounted under the dash.

Paul called for her again, this time playfully. "Amaaaandaaaa?"

Laughing, she reached under the instrument panel and snatched the receiver off the unit. She thumbed down the switch.

"Yesssss, Paul."

"*There* you are. I was getting worried."

"Bullshit, Paul."

His laughter was even cute coming from such a crummy speaker.

"You don't think I worry about you?" he asked.

"I think you know you don't have to worry."

"Oh, that's right. I forget that you're not some ordinary woman and all. A complete badass not to be messed with."

"That's right."

"How could I have forgotten such a thing?"

"I don't know. I thought you would have learned by now."

"I'm a slow learner."

"I believe it."

As she smiled, Paul laughed softly.

He said, "I hate that you're not up in the tower with me today."

She leaned back, propping her foot in the gap between the opened door and windshield. "Aw. Sounds like someone misses me."

"Someone definitely does. And it's *me!*"

Amanda laughed. "Well, I *suppose* I miss you, too."

"Holy shit! How hard was that?"

"How hard was what?"

"Admitting your weakness. I bet that tore you apart on the inside."

"My weakness? What are you talking about?"

"Wow and you gave it up. Just like that." He clucked his tongue. "That was easy."

"I didn't admit anything!"

"You admitted plenty."

"I can always retract the statement."

"No, no. I like the statement. It's nice to know that no matter how *tough, independent, and sexy* you are, I am what weakens you. In a good way."

She could hear his smile through the hand piece. "I never said any of that!"

"You said it, without words."

"All right, fine. I'll admit it. You rock my socks."

"*Yes!*"

Laughter tore out of her, bringing tears to her eyes. "Are you dancing in the tower?"

"You better believe it."

Amanda pictured him moonwalking back and forth in front of his tiny desk, a triangle-shaped smile wide on his face. Now she saw him still dancing but without the ranger uniform. His muscular legs tanned and smooth, his arms a perfect, tawny match. He was a bicyclist, so his body was always hairless and shiny, except for his head which had probably been gelled into spikes.

Then she remembered their boss's office was right

behind the radio table.

"Is George in there with you?" she asked.

"If he was, I'd make him dance with me!"

Amanda was relieved. "Thank God."

"I know. I'm not in any hurry to see him dance."

"Where is he?"

"Delivering some deer feed to the petting zoos."

There were two of them, spread a great distance apart through the mountains. She figured George would probably be tied up for most of the day just driving. Now she really wished she was in the tower with Paul. If she was, she might have been able to make that naked dance a reality.

She might have joined him.

Might have?

She'd have definitely joined him.

Paul continued. "He won't be back until late this afternoon."

"I was wondering why you were being so sweet to me."

"Hey—I would be sweet to you *even* if George *was* here. It's you who wants to keep us a secret, remember?"

Amanda felt an ache in her chest. He'd brought that up again. "For now." Her throat tightened. "Let's not get into that now."

"Yeah," he agreed. "Might turn into an argument."

There was no 'might' to it.

"I'm guessing you rang me for a reason other than to flirt with me."

"I did?" he asked.

He had her smiling, again. He was so good at that, better than anyone ever has been.

"Oh, right," he said. "You hadn't updated the booth with your location. You know the rules, young lady."

"Your rules or the state's?"

"The state, of course. I for one understand that you're a tough, independent woman."

She shook her head. "You're talking some major shit to me while being several miles away in the tower, aren't you?"

"You can't get me in here."

Amanda laughed, but tried to keep her tone more serious than what she actually felt. "I can be there real soon. Don't egg it on."

"All right, all right. I'll stop."

"I didn't say you had to stop. I like it."

It was Paul's turn to laugh. "Are you going to tell me where you are or not?"

"You know, if they would just install damn GPS in our vehicles, they would always know."

"But if they did that, it might put some of us out of a job."

That was always Paul's argument to the GPS units. She sighed. "I'm about eight miles past Miller's Quarry. Marker Six, Zone Four." She paused for him to freak out.

And he did. "All the way out there!? What the hell for?"

"I found an abandoned campsite, then tracked it to

some discarded trash. Nothing that shows it was our farmers, though."

"We both know they're out there somewhere." His voice sounded more annoyed than concerned. "But you can't spend all your time searching for them. You're treading on some scarcely traveled territory out there. I wouldn't even be able to get through it without a damn good map and compass. Do you have either with you?"

"Yep," she lied. "Both." There might a map in the glove compartment.

"You still shouldn't be that far out. George will shit if he finds out."

"I've been saying for months they're probably camped out near the gorge somewhere. That's about the only place with a thick enough blanket of trees to conceal them from the choppers. And we still haven't checked."

"They're probably spread out all over the damn mountains. There's a lot of ground out there that none of us have even seen yet."

"I know. And that's why I'm planning on *seeing* it."

Paul sighed. "This obsession of yours is not healthy."

"It's not an obsession."

That was a lie. She *was* obsessed and had been since Hillary Dent wandered into the ranger's station on Pine Ridge last year. Nineteen years old, she'd been lost in the woods for eleven days. They were nearing the point of calling off the search party. The volunteers had gone home, and the only ones allowed to search at that point were Amanda and Paul and even they were beginning to think the search was pointless.

But what the searchers—Amanda included—hadn't realized was the poor girl had not just gone camping with her family and somehow wandered away from them. She'd been abducted while swimming in a small basin while her parents and brother searched for a level place to set up the tents.

Hillary Dent had described her abductors as hillbilly mountain people, two guys and a girl. She'd believed they were all siblings. They'd taken her to an area where they were camping while gathering crop from their marijuana plants. Nicole had stated there were 'bags of the stuff' everywhere. When she was asked if she was certain it was marijuana, she'd answered matter-of-factly: 'Of course. Everyone knows what weed looks like."

"If it's not an obsession," Paul started, "then what is it?"

"Are you trying to say I'm wasting my time?"

"Hey—I never said that."

But Amanda had been speculating the same as Paul that perhaps the farmers had moved on and they just weren't out there to find anymore. Whenever she searched for them, she turned up nothing for her efforts. It was like they didn't even exist. A lot of folks wondered if Hillary was being completely honest with them.

The rape tests had come back positive. There was

no denying someone had violated her and held her captive for a couple days before she'd escaped.

Others hadn't been so lucky.

Amanda said, "And what about the missing person reports for the last three years? Tons of people—females—that went into the mountains and never came back out. I've been doing my research, buddy."

"You're right. There are a lot of people that have vanished without a trace, but not all of those are in our jurisdictions."

"They're close enough. Too close to be coincidental."

"All right. I'll give you that. But that's some very dense wilderness, and they might be anywhere. They could even have little harvests all over the forest. If someone happened to stumble across one while they were picking crop…"

"Yep. And if that someone happened to be female."

"Then our farmers would look at that as a bonus."

"Exactly. And it's not that they're *just* pot farmers. They're monsters. This deep in the hills, they think regular law doesn't apply to them. They need to be reminded that it does."

Paul groaned. "I love it when you talk sexy."

Amanda held back laughing, but not by much. "Stop. You're going to put me in a good mood."

"And that's wrong?"

She didn't respond.

"Listen. Since you're halfway up the damn mountain anyway, would you drive by the General

Campground?"

"And check on the campers that I signed in yesterday?"

"That's the idea."

Amanda checked her watch. It would take her half an hour to get there. "Okay. Just because I'm sweet on you, I will ride out of my way to do that. In this rough terrain, on tires that need to be changed."

"Now you're sweet on me? Wow, you really do miss me, huh?"

He sounded sincerely surprised. Maybe she should stop pretending as if his companionship wasn't treasured. It was what she looked forward to the most daily.

"Yeah," she said. "I'll check back in a few."

"Bye, my love!"

Smiling, she slapped the receiver back on the clip of the radio box, then leaned back in her seat. Staring through the windshield, she sighed. She really didn't want to take the time to drive by the campground. It would put her in a different section of the mountain, and she wanted to get to the gorge by early afternoon. With George being gone most of the day, she could make some serious distance without his knowledge.

But she'd told Paul she would do it, so that was what she would do.

A quick stop to make sure they put out their fires and cleaned up their trash.

Should only take ten minutes once she got there.

No problem.

Amanda pulled her door shut, buckled her seatbelt, then fired the engine. She eased away from the verge of the dirt pathway, steering the Jeep higher into the mountain and deeper into the woodland.

8

Megan continued her never-ending dash. Felt like she'd been running for hours, but she guessed that realistically it had been no more than ten minutes. She was tired and growing more sluggish with each step as she ducked under overhanging tree limbs, leaped over exposed roots and depressions in the soil.

She went around a large oak tree with billowy branches that offered heavy shade and shelter for her to hide under and take a short break. Huffing, she leaned against the uncomfortable, jagged tree bark. Her chest ached all the way through to her back. She felt a horrible pinch in her side.

She needed to check her wound. Raising her leg, she studied her calf. The bleeding had stopped, but now her leg looked as if she was wearing a red knee-high.

Megan smirked at the thought, then lowered her foot back to the ground.

Veneered in sweat, her skin shimmered under the summer sun. She ran a hand through her damp, tangled hair. Fingers became entwined in the knots, and she needed to tug her hand out to free them. Strands of hair dangled from her fingertips. As she pulled them off, she took a moment to study her surroundings.

Where the hell am I?

That same finger snuck into her mouth and she quickly began to gnaw at it. Earlier, she'd caused it to bleed, but right now she couldn't care less. She chewed on it as if it was a straw.

Megan looked around. Nothing but unending walls of trees was all she could see.

A subtle movement caught her eye. She looked around the tree, staring into the direction she'd come from.

Him.

His back was turned to her. And this gave her a small window of opportunity to flee. And she did. Quietly. Tiptoeing farther away, she hid behind another tree. She planted her back firmly against the rough bark, exhaled. Her vision was splotchy. She hadn't realized she'd been holding her breath this entire time.

Gnawing at her lip, she dared another look.

Now, the psychopath was investigating the tree she was at previously with his mask pressed against it, sniffing like a dog that has caught a scent.

She needed to move, but she couldn't with the risk of being spotted so high. A few horrendous moments passed before he finally looked away. She repeated the same trek as before, finding another tree even farther away to duck behind. Megan slowly exhaled. This time she counted to sixty in her head before chancing another look.

Angling her body sideways, she leaned over, aiming her eyes where she'd just been hiding.

But her view was blocked by a powerfully built torso.

Before she could let go of a scream, his hand latched hold of her throat. She was jerked to him. His stench was inhuman. She'd never smelled anything like it before—like sewage eaten and regurgitated on top of rotten meat.

Megan fought back. His grip tightened. Now she couldn't breathe at all. She began pounding on his chest with both fists. She struck him repeatedly with all she had. To her surprise his grip loosened. Air tried to push its way back into her lungs. It rushed in but still wasn't fast enough for Megan. She hacked, coughed. The interior of her mouth was caked in dry spit.

His hand made for another grab. As the L-shape of his opened hand came at her, she caught it with her teeth. They sank into the spongy patch of flesh between the thumb and forefinger. He groaned, showing pain. This fueled her more. If she could hurt him, she could beat him. She clamped harder, not stopping until both rows of teeth touched. Then she vigorously shook her head from side to side. She could feel the flesh rip away from his hand. Now, he was not screaming, but howling from behind his mask.

Megan turned her head and spat. A moist wad of bloody tissue thwacked the dirt with a wet slap.

The psychopath staggered back, holding his hand to his chest. Megan looked around for a weapon of some kind, quickly spotting something nearby—a broken limb, the girth of a parking pole. She grabbed it, using both hands to keep it steady as she hoisted the log-like branch over her shoulder. She swung like someone stepping up to the mound.

It was too late for him to attempt stopping her.

The club clobbered him in the back. He tensed up, dropping to his knees. She stepped around to the front of him, raised the club high above her head, and brought it down.

It cracked in half over the top of his skull.

His arms went limp by his side. Then he tumbled forward, landing hard on his chest. The machete bounced away from him.

Megan dropped the broken portion of the limb. She looked at the machete lying on the ground just feet from her. A much better weapon. She ran to it, snagging the massive blade by its handle. She couldn't lift it. It felt like trying to lift a small car.

Since the machete was much too heavy for her to carry, she pulled the hilt, dragging it across the ground in short, swift steps. Her new plan was that because she couldn't carry it, she would simply pick it up, then drop it—blade first—on the maniac's head.

The machete slipped through her sweaty fingers. It slapped the earth just a few inches shy of him. She was about to try again when his hand twisted around her ankle, squeezing so hard it popped. She painfully shrieked on her way down. When her rump slammed the ground, her teeth clacked together.

Her ankle hurt. So did her jaw and teeth.

He tugged.

Her buttocks skidded across the ground. Bumpy objects poked her. "Let go of me, dammit!"

She used her other foot to kick. It was a wild defense, blindly executed, and she hadn't expected to actually connect with anything. But to her surprise her foot landed perfectly on the nose of his mask. She heard a crack. Felt something crumble under her shoe. He stopped what he was doing, the shock slowly sinking in. His eyes narrowed into a scowl.

"Oh…shit…"

She should be gratified. Not only had she hurt him once, but twice. However, her pride was heavily cowed thanks to the rising fear from knowing she'd pissed him off.

He yanked her with such velocity that she dropped onto her back and zipped across the ground. Her shirt hiked up on her back. The grass scored her skin, leaving it burning and itchy.

Megan kicked with her free leg, catching him on the jaw. He tottered a bit but didn't fall or let go. She attempted three more times, and on the third conjunction of her foot against his face, he released her. She scooted back, getting out of grabbing range, and stood up. She took only a moment to regain her bearings before turning and launching herself even deeper into the woods.

Stealing a glance over her shoulder, she saw the maniac was on his knees. He looked to be observing his injured hand, the minute-sized wound that matched Megan's mouth.

She didn't know if she would get out of these woods alive.

9

There was a mangled tent straight ahead. Another tent sat practically untouched to the left. Amanda stood at the launch of the campsite, a glowering look of shock wrinkling her face.

Her eyes returned to the dead girl. She lay awkwardly on her stomach, but her face pointed at the sky.

Amanda bent at the waist, heaving nothing but air. This was her third attempt at vomiting. She'd skipped breakfast, so nothing was coming out. Her sides felt tight and achy, her stomach had cramped into knots, and the flat between her shoulder blades was sore.

Amanda looked at the girl once more. She couldn't stop looking. The girl's face was frozen in pure terror, mouth agape, her lifeless eyes two wraithlike orbs that seemed to stare through Amanda.

"God…"

She tried to absorb what she was seeing but it seemed impossible. Daring herself to move closer, she skulked to the broken body. Amanda drew her .45. Its familiar weight helped her feel better, to focus.

And it was ready to fire.

She scanned her surroundings. All seemed quiet. Unnaturally quiet. Whoever had done this had clearly moved on. She could sense it. Other than Amanda, no one alive was nearby.

She slowly kneeled by the girl. Even though it was pointless, she checked for a pulse. When her fingers grazed the spiraled, dough-like flesh of the dead girl's neck, she snatched her hand back as if it had been burned. The tips of her fingers felt as if she'd dipped them in ice water.

"Oh shit…oh shit…"

Panic hoped to invade her mind, conquering what small amount of practicality she'd managed to keep hold of after discovering such a brutal scene. She practiced slow breaths, hoping to calm her erratic nerves.

Struggling to stand, Amanda brushed her hand across her pants as if she could wipe away the feel of the girl's cold skin. She stepped around the body, making her way to the tent to her left.

Looming in on the front, she could see inside through the gaped flap. She spotted blood-soaked walls inside. She got down on one knee in front of the tent, using the barrel of her .45 to push the sagging flap aside, and peered inside.

There was *a lot* of blood, strewn about viscera, and a mutilated torso.

"Two bodies were all you found?" asked Paul.

Amanda sat in the SUV, the driver's side door propped open, and leaning stiffly forward. "Isn't two enough?"

"You know what I mean. There were three that went out there. No third person?"

"The other tent, which I believe belonged to the other girl, was demolished. But I didn't find any trace of her. I did a brief search of the grounds but turned up squat."

"Have you been to the turnoff to see if their car is there?"

"Not yet."

"She's out there somewhere."

"Exactly."

"I wonder if maybe she hightailed it."

"Why would she do that? She's probably been abducted."

"You don't think she might have been the one who killed the others?"

The image of the girl with the cranked neck sizzled in her mind. "Not a chance."

"You're sure?"

"Paul."

"All right, you're sure. I'll radio in for a chopper, see if I can get some rangers in from Shenowa to back us up."

Amanda felt a little better, but not much. "Sounds like a plan."

Paul's distorted voice came back, "In the meantime, hang tight. I'll be ringing you in a few minutes to let you know what's going on."

"I'll be here."

"*There.* You'll be *there*. Right? You're not going to take off and go looking around, right?"

"Paul—"

"—Promise me you'll stay there, okay?"

Amanda harrumphed. "Okay."

"Give me a few." Then he was gone.

Amanda hung up the receiver, shut her door, and fired up the engine. Then she drove off, ignoring Paul's request as she continued in the direction she'd been going.

10

Megan was no longer running, but staggering, hand clutched to her side as sharp pains pierced her abdomen. She was exhausted. Panting.

She knew he would pop back up but prayed it wasn't anytime soon. If he were to come now, she wouldn't have the strength to retaliate. She would surely die. Knowing this should have given her a sudden surge of energy, that jolt of power she needed. It gave her nothing. If she couldn't find the determination to fight for her survival, then she was already gone.

Right?

"Nope," she muttered, but wasn't convinced by her own voice.

Her skin was hot and sticky, and although she felt

as if she was leaking sweat from every pore of her body, she was hardly sweating at all. That meant she was well-past dehydration. Surprisingly, she wasn't hungry. Although she hadn't eaten in several hours, food was the farthest from her mind.

Rest. She needed rest. And some water if she could swing it.

Looking around, she didn't see any streams to drink from.

Seriously? This is the goddamn mountains and there isn't any water?

If she walked a little bit farther, she'd probably come across something, but she was just too tired to attempt it right now. The resting idea sounded like the better one now. But where could she? Just lying down right where she was walking would be a bad idea.

He'd spot me for sure.

For all she knew, he'd already spotted her and had been silently trailing her all this time. She glanced behind her, expecting to find him standing right there.

And he was.

Her heart jumped in her chest. She blinked and he was gone. Standing motionless, she stared into the woods. She debated whether he had really been there or not.

Her eyes were fucking with her. She *really* needed some rest.

Up ahead was a secluded spot, a heavy cluster of trees and wilting limbs for her to hide under. Some of the branches were nearly touching the ground.

A perfect place.

Megan hurried to the grove, hunkered down, and crawled under the limbs. Pine needles sighed across her arms. She went deeper in. Tall, willowy trees ringed around her. She found a spot, leaned against a tree, and hugged her knees to her chest. It had been a long time since she'd felt so sad and afraid that hugging her knees could make her feel at all safe.

She buried her face into the groove between her knees. The tears came right away, slurping against her eyes and skin. The morning played back in her head through a series of rapid images. When she'd gone to sleep last night, everything had been normal. Her life, her *boring* life had been ticking along as it always had. Dully. Enter Allison and Brian with a proposal, a weekend trip to the mountains—just like old times.

Forget about what ails ya! Allison had said, in a horrible attempt at an Irish accent.

Megan had been more than eager to go. She'd anticipated the trip with the same kind of excitement she got as a child counting down the days to Christmas. In a way, this trip was like Christmas. She was getting together with friends, doing something fun. And last night *had* been so much fun. They'd talked about old adventures and vowed that these excursions would become a ritual once again.

That idea's done.

As dead as her friends.

She hated she'd allowed herself to think such a thing.

Her mind drifted. Sleep unexpectedly came, putting all thoughts on hold.

11

Amanda kept the SUV creeping along, the hand on the odometer barely tapping the five. She rotated her gaze from the windshield to the driver's side window, out the passenger side, and repeating the never-ending cycle. All she wanted to find was a spark of human life, but all she'd seen thus far was expansive land with such thick huddles of trees her eyes couldn't infiltrate their luscious green fortresses.

Paul's voice exploded from the radio. She loosed a scream.

"Dammit, Paul!" Shaking it off, she snatched the radio. "Yeah?"

Paul's voice sounded even cracklier than earlier, and even then he'd been hard to understand. Because she was getting further and further away from the tower, her signal was waning.

"I've got some good news and some bad news."

"Let me hear the bad news," she said.

"The chopper is occupied. It's being used back at the state park to air lift someone to the hospital. Apparently, some old lady had a heat stroke trying to hike to Cemetery Ridge."

Amanda wasn't surprised. Too many attempted that complex hike, and usually suffered for it. "Wonderful. Is she okay?"

"The lady?"

"No, the chopper! Of course the lady."

"Ouch. Yes, they think she's going to be okay."

"Thank God for that. So what's the good news?"

"That was the good news."

"That she's going to be okay?"

"Yep."

"Fuck me sideways with a tire swing."

"I *did* manage to get us four more rangers from the state park. But it'll take two hours for them to reach Cunningham Point, which is where you need to meet them. I've also got calls into Brad and Sheena, even though they're off duty, hoping to get them to come in."

"Did you say Cunningham Point?"

"Yeah."

"Are they high? It'd take me nearly two hours just to *get* to that area. They could access the mountain paths from Bava's Bend and come up the back way and meet me near Carpenter's Caverns."

"What the hell are you doing heading towards the Caverns? They were condemned, remember? Too many tunnel collapses."

"I'm not heading to them, but I can be, and besides, I'm not planning to trudge through them. They could meet me at the old turnoff. It would cut an hour off their drive time and mine."

Paul sighed heavily into his end of the microphone. The speaker crackled like wadding tin foil. "Not everyone has your balls, Amanda. That's some intense terrain and not many people can handle it, nor do they want to try."

"For petesake…"

"I'm just relaying the message."

"Well, relay this back to *them*. Tell them if they want to come in their way then fine. But also inform them not to wait on me because I'm not going to meet them there. I'm already deep in, and don't know how much better I can do on wheels. I might have to switch over to foot before too long and search somewhere other than the road."

"You didn't wait at the camp like I asked, did you?"

"What do *you* think?"

The speaker fizzed again from another heaved sigh.

Amanda ignored his reaction. "We're missing one of the girls. If the farmers have taken her, then I'm probably already too late as it is…"

"You don't even know for sure that's who it is. You don't even know for sure if they exist at all. You're going off of one girl's testimony. She could have been lying."

"Whether that girl lied last year or not is irrelevant.

We're missing at least one girl, *now*! And again, I do *not* believe she is the one responsible for the death of the other ones at the camp. She just doesn't have the strength…to do what was done to them."

"Okay, Amanda, okay. But what if you waste all this time searching for the pot farmers, when you should be searching for the missing girl? Do you get what I'm trying to say?"

She did. And he made perfect sense. "Yes, but I have a feeling if I find her, I'll find them."

"What if you're wrong? What if by hunting those areas you think these farmers might be hiding, you completely miss where the girl actually is?"

Again, he was right. She hadn't thought of that possibility, either.

"Hold on," said Paul. The CB clicked and went silent. He'd switched lines.

She pushed down the button on hers. "Paul?" He was gone. Something had come up, and he must be talking to someone else. She'd have to wait for him to come back.

Continuing the sluggish pace, she kept her eyes scanning everything. Maybe she should go on and park and start hiking. She had plenty of daylight to march *into* the woods, and a decent flashlight with a big bulb for when the sunlight left her. She tried to remember what all food supply she had in her bag. Seemed like there was trail mix, beef jerky, and a couple bottles of water. That would be enough for a few miles of hiking.

She'd been heading west since leaving the campsite.

She'd found no trace of the campers' car on her way in, so she was pretty confident she was heading in the right direction.

But what if she wasn't looking in the right spots?

It was doubtful that if the missing girl had been taken, her abductor would have kept to the main path where anyone could drive along and spot them. Not that there was much risk out this far, maybe once every few months would that happen. Still, the chances of them keeping to the road were slim.

Paul's voice came back. "Just got word that a medic unit is going to the camp to retrieve the bodies. Investigators have been dispatched to examine the scene."

"Okay. Good."

"I wish you were there to greet them."

"They won't need me to explain what happened out there. When they see it, they'll know."

And they'll be just as scared as I am.

12

Megan heard the soft crunch of a footstep. Under the tree, her head down, she peeked over her forearm. The crunch repeated in a short succession, growing slightly louder as it neared.

Her body went rigid. She listened to the evident approach of footsteps growing closer.

Oh God, please no. Don't let him find me. God please...

"Megan?"

Her breath choked in her throat.

"Megan? Where *are* you?"

Allison?

"Where are you? I'm worried!"

"Al?"

"Megan!"

How was this possible? Allison was dead.

Wasn't she?

Had to be. There was no way she could have survived that. No way.

But maybe…

"Megan!"

Alive or not, she needed to stop shouting.

"Al? Over here."

The soft crunch changed to a heavy patter as feet tore through the brush. The limbs around her began to shake. An opening formed in the green and her best friend, the girl she thought had been slain right in front of her, emerged from the trees.

Allison looked just as mangled as she had when Megan left her at the camp. At least now her face was on the correct side of her body, save a lumpy mess of loose flesh dangling around her neck like a skin scarf about to fall off. Her lips had gone purple and crackly. She had dark circles around her eyes that made it look as if she were wearing sunglasses.

The bloodstains on her skin had turned from red to light brown, coagulated patches that looked like old, streaked paint. "There you are," she said, getting down on one knee. As she did her body made awful popping sounds. Her head collapsed sideways with an arthritic crackle. "Whoops." She gripped a handful of her tangled, straw-like hair, and pulled her head back up. "What are you doing back here?"

"Huh-hiding…" Her face scrunched up. "How…is it possible?"

"What?"

"You're alive. How…?" She held up her hand, waved it up and down to indicate the damage done to her. "How?"

"I pretended to be dead, just like I did the first time. I think he believed it. Wouldn't you?"

Megan looked at the bulges in Allison's neck pressing against her overextended skin. That had to be bones, broken bones jutting in multiple directions.

I've lost my damn mind.

Allison studied Megan with caution. "You are glad to see me, aren't you?"

Of course she was. That was a stupid question. But seeing her like this? No. She wasn't happy about what happened to her friend because Megan was too frightened to come out of the tent to help her.

If you would have, you'd look just like her.

Then it should have been like that. Both of them should be a mess.

Megan realized she hadn't answered Allison. "You know I'm happy you're okay."

"I'm not *okay*. I'm alive, though."

The hell you are. I've gone bonkers. Completely bonkers! This is the moment I'll always remember as the time I went batshit crazy.

Allison motioned for her to stand up. "Come on, let's go."

"Where?"

"To the car. I found it." She thrust her chin in a direction separate from where she'd been heading, and her head craned back with a snap. "Dammit. This is annoying." She repeated the grab-and-pull procedure to get her head situated correctly.

Grimacing, Megan stared at Allison in all her

disfigured glory. There was no chance she could have simply waited for the maniac to get out of sight, go find the car, and come back to tell Megan about it.

Allison continued talking. "We were way off. Sorry about that. I thought I could have found it, but we were moving in the wrong direction. We have to go this other way. It's a shortcut."

"A shortcut?"

"Yeah." Allison looked at her in that accusatory way again. "Don't you believe me?"

"I find it a little hard to believe you walked all that distance and back in such a short time looking like..."

"Looking like what?"

"Like the way you look."

"Hmm." Allison crossed her arms. They crunched as they folded across her puffy, gray-colored breasts. "The way I *look*, huh? Real nice. I'm here to help you and you make fun of how messed up I am. Don't you think I'm already self-conscious enough about it? I thought you of all people wouldn't judge me. That's great, Meg, just great."

Megan sighed. Now she'd pissed off a figment of her shattered imagination. "You're right, I'm sorry. I shouldn't have said that."

"You're fucking right you shouldn't have. Quit being a bitch and believe me when I tell you I can get you out of here."

Perhaps she should trust Allison.

This is crazy.

And it was. She briefly entertained the idea she

might be sleeping, or most likely, dead. Maybe Allison was here to lead her to Hell. But she didn't think so. The elements were way too tangible. She could smell the woods, the watermelon scent of the grass, and the sweetness of the pines. The breeze on her skin was soft and cool like tiny kisses. Birds chirped with no care. Leaves rustled in the trees like whispering voices.

She was awake. Allison was here. And this was happening whether Megan wanted it to be or not.

"I'm sorry," she told Allison. "I'll stop being a bitch."

Allison smiled at that. "Good. Now get up." She staggered away, her head clanking to the right.

Groaning, Megan leaned up, then crawled under the sagging limbs. Their gaunt tips scratched across her arms. Sweat seeped into the abrasions and burned as if a lit match had been placed against her skin. The gash on her calf stung as it stretched and pulled with her movements.

Resurfacing from her hiding spot, she stood up and stretched. Her cramped muscles relaxed a little, but they still felt hard and achy. It was brighter out here, and she needed to narrow her watery eyes against the blazing sunlight. This would be the perfect time for the maniac to pounce, unable to see him if he came at her. As she pushed herself upright, using the tree to help her stand, she expected the heavy clout of his machete across her back.

It didn't come.

She rubbed her eyes, smearing the squint-caused

tears. From where she stood, she looked around. She didn't see the man but wouldn't be surprised if he was there. By now, he'd probably become a professional at blending into the woods.

"Are you going to stand there all day?" said Allison, stepping around from a tree a few feet away. "Let's *go*."

Leaning against the tree, Megan nodded. She winced as she shoved herself forward with a shoulder.

Allison's nose wrinkled as if she smelled something foul. "You don't look so hot yourself, Meg. He do that to you?"

"Yeah."

"Wow. He's a strong one, that's for sure. Just look at what he did to me!" Allison chuckled. "You got off lucky, though."

"For now."

Allison nodded. "Yep. For now."

Megan joined Allison and together they started walking.

13

They trundled along in silence. Megan dragged her feet, moving as if on autopilot. Her head hung low. She watched her shoes, one stepping, the other vanishing, then they repeated. Nothing registered beyond the small space of ground that she could see.

Allison's body crunched beside her with each jolt of a footstep. Each time sounded like she had stepped on a puddle of acorns. Megan still couldn't accept the fact that her best friend had survived such a brutal attack.

There's no way she survived. You're bonkers!

Megan frowned.

Maybe I am dead after all.

She couldn't accept that, either.

Wondering what time it was, Megan looked at the sky as if she could somehow ascertain it that way. The only conclusion she could attain by doing this was it was daylight.

"Look at that," said Allison.

"Huh?"

Allison had stopped walking. She was looking to the left of them. Megan followed her line of sight through the woods to a small clearing in the trees. It took a moment to train her eyes.

A shack—more like an extemporized hut—had been constructed amongst the trees. Covered in leaves and vines, the shoddy structure looked as if it had been haphazardly pieced together by whatever means necessary. And it seemed as if those supplies had been scarce.

But it was something. Shelter. And Megan couldn't help feeling a slight trace of alleviation.

"Thank God," said Allison.

Megan said, "Do you think anyone lives in there?"

"They might." Allison was already heading towards it.

"What are you doing?"

"Going to knock on the door."

"No, wait…"

Allison stopped, gripped her hair, and twisted her head around so she could look at Megan. "What for?"

"We can't just walk up to it. What if someone's inside?"

"Isn't that the point of going to knock?"

Megan huffed. "I don't think it's a good idea. There's no telling what kind of person lives in there."

"*If* anyone even does."

That was a chance Megan didn't want to take, but

before she could retort, Allison was already heading to it. Her head was back on right; however, she was still gripping it by the hair.

Megan jogged to catch up. There weren't any trails out here, so they were walking right through the high grass. She looked down, making sure she wasn't about to step down on any snakes. Copperheads were the most common around these parts, but she'd seen more than one rattler in the mountains. And she'd learned the slimy shits loved tall grass. You never knew they were out here until you were right on top of them and, by then, you were feeling a double shot of needle-like stings as venom was injected into your bloodstream.

With everything else that had happened so far, she expected any time she would feel that whipping bite.

Thankfully, that never happened.

Allison and Megan reached the hut.

There was no door, only a sagging tarp. As Megan examined further, she realized the entire structure had been assembled from tarps and black plastic. Resembling an army tent more than an actual house or dwelling of some kind, the trees around it had been used as posts, the tarps and plastic wrapped around.

"Some place, huh?" said Allison.

"Quiet. Someone might hear you."

"Oh, please. Who do you think would actually live in there?"

"No one I'd like to meet."

"Whatever. You know as well as I do this place is empty."

"I don't care. Let's keep moving."

Allison turned on a creaky neck to see her. "You're being a bitch again."

"Why? Because I'm disagreeing with you?"

"That's one of the reasons."

"Jesus."

"You never know what we might find in there. Maybe something we can use."

"And maybe someone else just as fucked up as the maniac that did this to us."

With a sigh, Allison took the crinkly curtain in her hand. "Do I have to do *everything?*" She started to gradually pull the tarp back.

As Megan watched, she sucked her finger back into her mouth and nervously chewed on the tip. By this point, she no longer cared how gnawed up it had become.

The flap was opened enough that Allison could enter, so she did. Slipped right through the space and vanished as if sucked into a black hole.

Megan hesitated. "Al?"

Nothing.

"Answer me, Al."

A few seconds passed and there still was no response.

"Dammit, Al!"

The tarp snapped back. Megan started with a squeal.

Allison poked her coiled neck out. "What's your deal?"

"Why didn't you answer?"

"I was trying to check it out."

"What'd you find?"

"Can't tell much. It's too damn dark. My eyes didn't have time to adjust."

"Was anyone inside?"

"Not that I could tell. I'm sure we would have heard about it by now if there is."

"Ready to move on?"

"No."

"Why not?"

Annoyed, she said, "Because we haven't searched the place yet. Might be some stuff we can use." Her head disappeared behind the canvas.

"Damn." Megan was going to have to go inside. Tugging the tarp back, she checked over her shoulder for the maniac. He wasn't back there anywhere, just a barrier of trees. But she could feel that he was nearby. Somehow, she sensed him. Did he sense her?

Probably.

At least this little hut offered some type of concealment.

Hardly anything to celebrate.

She took a deep breath, pulled back the tarp, then slipped inside.

The luminance from outside dematerialized, shrouding her in darkness as if a rock had been pushed in front of the opening. She noticed stabs of light coming from tiny holes in what she guessed was meant to be the ceiling.

And it reeked in here. Making a face, she cupped a

hand over her nose and mouth.

"Oh yuck," said Allison from ahead.

Megan strained her eyes and could just vaguely see a paler shape moving about the blackness. She headed towards her. Leaves carpeted the ground and crunched like wadded paper each time a foot came down.

Her eyes began to adjust. She could see a little better. Not much, but she could make out shapes and objects. She spotted a table to her left covered with a filthy sheet. To the right was a makeshift cot on the ground. Sheets had been bundled up for a mattress with an old, yellowed pillow at the top.

Even further in, she found a pile of soiled laundry—more blankets and various clothes as high as Megan's waist. She moved past it and the smell became much stronger. It brought tears to her eyes, and she could taste it on her tongue.

Her shoe tapped against something. There was a tinny thump. She looked down, finding a tin bucket at her feet where the tarps met, signaling she'd reached the end of the housing. Dried fecal matter crusted the insides of the bucket. A hole had been cut in the bottom. She could see a narrow conduit leading out from behind the bucket and continuing under the tarp, probably to a manmade latrine outside.

Megan gagged. She coughed behind her hand.

Enough!

She was ready to get out of here. "All right, it's time to…" Looking around, she didn't see Allison anywhere. "Al?" No response.

Had she slipped out?

Hurrying to the front flap, she brought it open. Brightness splashed into the darkened space.

Squinting against the sunlight, she noticed movement farther out in the woods. She blinked against the tears misting her eyes. Half-blinded, she began to make out a smear of a shape heading towards her. At first, she thought it might be Allison. Then she realized the color was all wrong. Allison had been wearing pastel-hued pajamas, and these were much darker. The person was larger in size. And carried something in his hand.

Something big.

Wide-eyed, she gasped, "Oh shit!"

It was *him*!

Oblivious to her, he was heading in her direction. She dropped the flap, stumbling back inside. Panning her head this way and that, she searched for a place to hide. All she saw were leaves, a clothed table, and a pile of rubbish.

Megan chose the rubbish.

She darted for the dungy fabrics and dropped to her knees. Grimacing, she dug her hands into the damp pile. Her plan was to burrow her way in, then curl into a ball and hope he wouldn't notice her.

Maybe he'll walk right by here and not come in.

Yeah, right. This is his place. I should've known.

Allison had led her here, then vanished on her. Where was she now?

Megan got her arms into the soggy mound up to her

shoulders, and pulled back a section, unveiling a rotted corpse underneath. She almost yelped like a dog that had been stepped on, but bit down on her bottom lip to keep her mouth closed. The cry came out as a muffled squeal.

The corpse had once been a female. The hair matched Megan's own in color, but not style. She had hollow sockets for eyes and a gnarled, frozen grin. The body was naked, colored like driftwood, with shriveled breasts that looked like rotten tomatoes.

Megan was stunned. She no longer wanted to hide, not with a corpse. But what choice did she have?

None.

She glanced at the front, expecting to see him barging in, but he wasn't there. Not yet. Any moment now she would hear the rustle of the tarp being drawn back.

Megan turned around, squirmed her rump against the corpse as if about to sit on its lap, and started piling soiled clothing on top of her. The moldy, rotted stench of the fabric, combined with the corpse's odor made her gag.

Just as she had pulled a layer over her head, making a sort of peephole through the clothing, the tarp up front was yanked back. A bracket of harsh light shot through the tight expanse. He stood in the doorway, a darkened silhouette against the effulgent sun.

She could tell he knew something wasn't right. From the entranceway, he looked around, scanning the interior from one side to the other. Megan was submerged in the shadows and disgusting clads piled on top of her. All that showed of her was a narrow slit of her eyes and bridge of her nose.

He doesn't see me.

Finally, he let the tarp fall, choking off the daylight. He moved through the hut, making his way to the table. He yanked the cover off, letting it flutter to the ground.

The table's surface was arrayed with countless weapons and tools. Megan also saw some rope, wire, tape, and various other instruments she couldn't even identify.

Good Lord.

Next to the table was an old rickety chair. It did not appear to be in such shape that it could support a child, let alone a man of his size, but he sat down regardless. Astonishingly, it held him.

He placed the machete on the table, then began rummaging through the mess cluttering the top of it. He found an old red rag, stained black with oil or most likely something else. He tore off a long parcel, tossed the rest back on the table, then proceeded to wrap the wound on his hand. When it was nice and tight, he knotted it and was done. He flexed his fingers a few times.

Megan could hear his fuming breaths even from back here. Seeing him aid his wound brought on a feeling of retribution. She wondered why he'd come here. Sure, bandaging himself was a reason, but she doubted it had been enough to pull him away from the pursuit. For all he knew, she was still out there, running around the woods. Maybe she'd even gotten the authorities and they were combing the woods to find him.

They're not.

And he knew it, too. The reason he'd taken this little break from the chase was because he knew that he could. There was no worry that Megan would get away and that meant there was no rush to find her.

Defeat channeled through her. She might as well clamber out from under this sodden mound of filth, go over to where he sat, and tap him on the shoulder to announce her surrender.

He grabbed a grinding wheel and his machete. Then he chafed the hefty blade with the grinder in slow thrusts. Sparks popped around him like fireflies as he sharpened the machete even more. With each flash, the room brightened a bit, casting Megan in its feeble gleam.

She scooted down, trying to hide herself more without attracting his attention.

It didn't work.

He whipped his head around, having caught a flicker of her movement in the corner of his eye. He glared into the darkness a moment. Then he tossed the grinder on the table, and slowly stood up.

Seeing him rise, Megan gently situated her head against the corpse in hopes it would shield him from seeing her. Her nose was pushed in the dry hair. It smelled faintly of dead flowers. She could see mites crawling through the tangled locks, hordes of them. They marched onto her nose, their tiny feet tickling, and threatening to make her sneeze.

She could hear the crunch of the maniac's boots on the dirt floor as he approached the pile, but she could no longer see him. She wasn't visible behind the corpse. A few moments that felt endless passed, and the scrape of him shoving the machete back into the sheath at his hip broke the uncomfortable silence.

Then she heard the padding of his steps as he walked away. It sounded like he was heading back to the front. Maybe he was leaving.

Megan dared a peek. She slowly peeped over a withered-gray shoulder.

There was a pause when he reached the tarp. He gave one last look over his shoulder, then exited.

The room was still for several beats.

Eventually, Megan maneuvered the corpse down to the ground so gingerly it made no sound. She began to stand as if trying to find her footing on ice. Her eyes stayed fixed on the front. Knee-deep in the laundry, she lifted a leg out and placed it on the ground outside the mess.

Behind her the tarp imploded.

Like a portal opening to a bedazzling dimension, light suddenly engulfed her. Megan screamed as two beefy arms hugged around her and pulled her kicking and screaming through the back.

Megan writhed and fought to no gain. Shrieked with all her throat could produce, and he didn't let go.

Once she was on the outside, the hold on her went away. She fell. A cloud of dust wafted out from under her when she landed hard on her side.

She gasped for breath between hacking coughs. He towered over her, savoring this. She watched him through the tangled tresses of her hair. He seemed to relish her suffering. She would swear she saw glee in his beady black eyes.

He stepped over her legs, grabbed each foot by the ankle, and dragged. She flipped onto her stomach, pawing at the ground, pulling out clumps of grass with clotted dirt bottoms as she tried to keep hold of something. All she really could do was allow herself to be hauled off, but she continued to fight as if she actually had a chance at escape.

There was no hope, and she was aware of this, but she slammed her fists down on the ground just the same.

14

Growing irritated, Amanda steered the Jeep to the berm of what she guessed counted as a road. The road had gradually tapered until becoming a narrow horse path, a penciled line of gravel and dirt through tall money-green grass.

Engine idling, she crossed her arms on the steering wheel, planting her head into the fold.

And groaned.

"Amanda, you there?"

Paul. His voice, crackly and thin, resonated from the radio. It was good hearing him, always, but right now she was tired of getting his updates. Each conversation had ended with him more disappointed with her than the last. She didn't like it when he was upset and couldn't figure out why it bothered her so much when he was. No other guy ever made her worry like that.

Maybe he's the one.

"Shit," she muttered. She'd always promised herself there would never be a *one*.

And when he found out she was even deeper into the mountain, he would probably shit his pants.

Without raising her head up, she groped for the receiver, found it, then pulled it to her and held the switch down. She had to slip it under the steering wheel to get it to her mouth. "Yeah?"

"Hey."

"Hey back."

"Are you okay?"

"Dandy, you?"

"Been better. Where are you? Do I even want to know?"

"Probably not."

"Well, I have to know whether I want to hear it or not."

"I'm not exactly sure, somewhere past Wiseman's Ridge."

"Jesus H. Christ, Amanda. You're going to get yourself lost."

"I'll be fine."

"Listen, Amanda, there are Marshals here, and they want you back at the tower right away. Apparently there's more going on than even we know. News about the murders traveled fast, and apparently the FBI is getting involved."

"What the hell?"

"I'm as confused as you are, but they demanded that you get back here so you can talk to the agent." There was some indistinct chatter in the background, then Paul added, "And they have questions of their own."

Now she was mad. It was hearing them spoon-feeding Paul every word he was saying to her. She pictured two overweight men packed into their cowboy threads, smelling like old cigarette smoke with brushes of beards that they never shaved, yet never seemed to grow more than a whisker.

She might have actually turned the Jeep around and driven the nearly three-hour ride back to the tower if it weren't for them telling Paul to add that little incentive at the end.

"Paul?" she said.

"Yeah?" There was a hint of worry in his voice. He must know what she planned to say next.

"Tell those marshals to go fuck themselves, and when that FBI agent gets there, tell him I said to watch them and join in if he wants to."

Paul sighed through the speaker so heavily it sounded like he was somewhere with massively gusting winds. There was some rustling and clicking sounds.

When a voice came back on, it did not belong to Paul. She recognized the kind of tone it had right away. This was someone she should not be trying to piss off. He was one of those legitimate badasses, the kind that had probably seen a lifetime of mayhem and had caused just as much himself. And all he said was, "Amanda Carpenter?"

"Yes," she said back in the same mysterious way.

"I'm Federal Marshal Ron Lamberson. And I am

not requesting for you to come back to the tower, I am *ordering* you to, and if you do not oblige, then not only will you lose your job, but you will be escorted off this mountain in shackles. Are we understanding each other?"

"Crystal clear. But I think there was some confusion."

"Oh?"

"Yeah. Because I told you to go fuck yourself, and you're on the horn still talking to me." She heard Paul groan in the background. "Now, I don't know what the hell I could possibly do for you back there when I'm out here trying to get answers. Those bodies were fresh enough that the person or persons responsible couldn't have gotten too far away."

"We need to have a moment where we can sit, and I can explain some things you might want to know."

"Tell me now, asshole!"

"All I will say is those areas you're in are the Bermuda Triangle of the mountains. People go in and never come out."

"I already knew that."

"I don't think you understand the severity, Ms. Carpenter, so if you would, please come back to the tower before it's too late."

"Are you threatening me?"

"I believe you heard my threats and that was not one of them. So, will you come back willingly?"

Amanda considered it only for a moment. "Nah. I politely decline your invite."

"Ms. Carpenter." Now there was clear frustration in his voice. "If you—"

"If this girl is still alive, then all that me trekking back to the tower is going to do is provide more time for her to be raped, killed, or both. If I can prevent that from happening…then I'm going to."

"Ms—"

"I'm done talking to you. And I'm killing radio contact." She took a deep breath. She knew this would cause him some problems back in the tower, but she felt it had to be said as well. "Paul, I know you can hear me. I do need you. I love you. And hopefully when this is over, you'll still want to be with me."

She tossed the receiver. It smacked the instrument panel, then dropped to the floor, stretching the coiled cord attaching it. As the fuzzy sounds of frantic movement played from the tiny speaker, she gripped the tiny knob on the radio between her forefinger and thumb. Then she shut it off, killing those in the tower's agitated retorts.

A heavy blanket of silence fell over the Jeep. She felt awful for how she'd acted, but at the same time, greatly relieved. She wasn't letting them pull her away from this. And why had they tried? She was already so far into the search, why make her come back now.

Easy. They knew something she didn't. And they wanted her away from whatever was going on out here.

What are they trying to hide?

And she felt bad because of what she'd said to Paul at the end. She knew he would catch some serious flack for it, but she also thought he was probably glad to have heard it. After the initial shock and the ribbing ended, George would forgive him for shitting where he ate, but she knew she was pretty much done being a ranger. Whenever she did decide to head back to the tower, it would be to collect her pink slip, clean out her locker, and turn in the gun and Jeep.

She'd miss the Jeep. She rubbed her fingers along the soft, rubbery skin of the steering wheel, and smiled. "I'll miss you most of all, scarecrow." Then she turned off the engine, taking away what little remained of the unnatural noise. All she heard now was the whisper of the woods, a subtle, almost secretive breathing that you only perceived in deep isolation.

She wanted to sit here and enjoy it longer, but she couldn't. Amanda removed the keys from the ignition, and as she climbed out, she slid them into the pocket of her tight-fitting khakis. Removing the ranger's shirt, she tied it around her waist by the sleeves. Then she checked that she had her gun, and two spare clips. She hoped she wouldn't need any more bullets because this was all she had.

Amanda walked around to the back, opened the gate, and grabbed her backpack. It was heavy on her shoulders, trying to pull her back. She shrugged, adjusting the straps so they weren't so tight. That made it better.

She shut the gate, then walked around to the driver's door, and pushed down the auto-lock button. Four locks clicked in synchronicity.

Amanda stepped onto the road, throwing the door shut in stride. She examined the woods to the left of the car. The camping area was back near Cunningham. If the missing woman was moving west, away from the turnoff, then she should be heading this direction.

This has to be the right way. I would have seen her anywhere else.

Not in the woods.

No, not there. But if I enter right here, and circle back around. I just might cut them off. Surely I'm ahead of them. They're obviously moving on foot. I might just run right into them.

That seemed very likely, and her mind was made up. She scanned the still forest one more time, then marched on.

15

A loud clangor resounded. Megan shrieked in crucial agony as the nail was driven inward through her wrist. A thin line of blood streamed down her arm. Half an inch of the rounded head protruded from her skin.

Another nail was pressed to her wrist beside the preceding one. Then the psychopath revved back the hammer and drove it home with a wet, splintering plunge.

Megan screamed again, tears spewing from her eyes. She had hoped by now she couldn't feel any more pain, but it seemed like it had increased with each blow of the hammer.

Her left hand, already pinned to the tree above her head, was bruised and bleeding warm sticky torrents down her arm. With both hands tacked there, her elbows stuck out on each side, giving her a human arrow shape.

He gave her arms a mighty tug. They were secure. She wasn't going anywhere.

Fighting off hyperventilation, she watched him swagger over to a campfire site. Rocks circled a stash of blackened branches of a previous fire. A flat grate had been mounted above the sticks and sitting on top of it was an old cast-iron frying pan.

The man stepped around the fire pit and skulked away from Megan.

When she saw where he was heading a fresh scream rose in her throat. Blinking away tears, she could see hammered to the other tree, in an identical pose, was a corpse. Fully clothed in hiking attire, she looked to have been here for quite some time. Not entirely decomposed, there was plenty of evidence she had once been a lovely girl. Her skin was as gray as cigarette ash, and her eyes had recessed into her skull. Wrinkled eye lids showed the dull whites of her eyes. They looked to have fossilized into Ping-Pong balls. Lips had peeled back, exposing two rows of perfect teeth on a slack jaw stuck in a silent scream. She'd had a large pair of breasts that now looked like rotten melons.

The psychopath ripping a piece off the dead girl's shirt snapped Megan out of the trance she was being pulled into. She shook her head to clear the mind fog, then attempted to move her arms. She squealed at the pain blasting down her arms and into her chest. It made her stomach feel like she'd been punched there. Her head snapped to the left, gazing past her blood-deluged arms.

And she saw the exhibit.

Her cries stopped flat. The girl was something she could understand missing when she was dragged into this section of the woods. She'd been fighting with her best efforts to free herself when he'd pinned her to the tree. She'd kept resisting his attacks while ramming nails the length of unsharpened pencils through her wrists with a rusted claw hammer.

But this other thing…?

How did I not see that?

Displayed like macabre lawn ornaments was a stock of corpses, all shapes, sizes, and sexes. In myriad positions, some were hammered and bound around a post, merged into a collage of grotesque art. Others had been planted with stakes lodged up their asses and the tops pushing out through their stretched-open mouths.

Megan realized right before it happened that she was losing all control of herself. She heard horrible, glass-shattering shrills reverberating all around her. When she realized they were coming from her, she cried even harder.

Acting as if she weren't there at all, he crouched at the stick pile, and stuffed the torn fabric between the twigs. He stuffed a hand into a pocket and tugged out a small box. Shaking it, the box made scraping noises. *Matches.* He took one out, striking it with the tip of his thumb. A tiny flame popped up, then he lowered the match down to the cloth, igniting it. The flames rose swiftly, licking the grate and slowly heating the iron pan on top.

Megan managed to bring her emotions down a few notches as he stood up with a slight groan. He sounded like someone who was getting to the age where he couldn't comfortably handle being in certain positions for extended periods of time.

She watched him remove the small knife from the siding on his thigh. This blade was angled, curving up to the point.

For carving.

Her eyes widened. She looked past him to the dead female occupying the other tree. She skimmed down the body like a panning camera, stopping at the thigh where jagged chunks had been removed. A stripe of bone stuck out from the dried-up meat like a drainage ditch in sinking soil.

Megan looked at the man. He was almost to her, the curved blade clutched in his hand. "No, no please don't. Please…"

Waving the blade to taunt her, he inched closer.

"Why are you doing this to me? Just…*kill* me. Get it over with!"

He joined her at the tree, putting the blade under her chin. She stopped shaking, her words died, but she didn't stop trying to supplicate with her eyes. She'd always been good at that, even as a kid. It worked on her daddy whenever he tried to be firm.

It wasn't working now.

Through the torn holes of his patched mask, his eyes glowered at her. Appetitive flair haunted his pupils. In them, Megan could foresee his next move.

And she wasn't surprised when he lowered the blade. Glided it down her chest, between her breasts, nudging her stomach, and resting it on her thigh.

"Don't...don't...please..."

He angled the blade against her flesh and sawed into her thigh.

Megan thrashed back her head to shout at the sky. It felt like sharpened ice serrating her thigh. She'd thought the slice on her calf had hurt, but it couldn't compare to this...she didn't think anything possibly could.

When the maniac gripped a handful of her meat and ripped it away from her leg, she realized she was wrong.

Megan nearly lost consciousness. Her vision turned dim and splotchy, as if she'd been staring at the sun for an hour and entered a dark room. Her weight sagged. Her hands pulled against the nails and a fresh tendril of pain pulled her back so she could watch him carrying a slab of her thigh over to the pan and toss it on.

It sizzled as it began to cook. Thin plumes of smoke curled up from the cooking meat.

Her leg felt broken, although the bone was fine. And she was so hungry that the smell of her frying meat made her stomach grumble, then it quickly soured when it realized what had pinged its attention.

16

Amanda, careful and vigilant, trooped onward. She looked around as she moved, turning to spy any noise she heard. Her gun was drawn, ready to fire. She stopped frequently to rub her sweaty hands on her pants. She could feel sweat trickling between her breasts, making her itch. She was tempted to stop and use her ranger shirt to dry her chest but didn't want to take the time away from her walk.

The sun had already begun its move. As afternoon ticked onward, the honey-colored blob would continue to shift until dropping out entirely. She assumed she had three, maybe four hours until the trees choked out the sun completely. She'd be moving in total darkness, although the sun wouldn't have completely set yet.

That's why I brought the flashlight.

But how long would the batteries hold out? She didn't want to be traipsing around out here with nothing to see by. She might just march her stubborn ass right off a ridge and careen a mile or so down to her death.

A lot of help she'd be if that happened.

Someone ducked behind the trees ahead of her. She clearly saw a head and flapping of hair. Amanda jogged to where she'd seen them.

A branch was lightly swaying as if someone had bumped it.

I did see someone.

But not who she thought it was. There was no way she could have seen *her*.

My eyes are playing tricks.

The heat, the stress, and the lack of food and water she'd had today. She was exhausted, maybe a little dehydrated. That could explain why she was seeing things that couldn't be real.

That girl was dead. Her head had been left on her shoulders the wrong way. She'd seen the poor girl herself, even touched her rippled neck. Felt the broken bones prodding the skin. Suddenly it felt as if she could feel that cold dough touch on her fingertip once again. She extended her finger, then quickly wiped it on the tank top.

She'd just seen that same girl, looking just as dead as she had earlier, moving around on her own.

Despite it being a record-breaking summer day, Amanda shivered.

There was a crunching sound that a foot might make beyond the barrier of trees.

"Hello?"

No one responded to her call.

She felt little legs scurrying all over her arms. She went to wipe them off but found her skin was clean. The feeling was still there, however there were no bugs.

Enough of this. You didn't see her!

Amanda stopped, staring at the flank of trees. She'd know for sure if she kept going.

No one was over there.

Let's prove it, then.

Taking a deep breath, she shoved her way through the branches.

And saw the girl again several yards up. Only for a flash of a moment, then she went to Amanda's left, disappearing around the backside of another tree.

Hurrying to the tree, Amanda didn't see her, but knew this was the direction she'd gone. Amanda followed, hoping that she hadn't lost her mind and was allowing her insanity to lead her deep into these woods to vanish with all the rest.

But if you haven't lost your mind, where does that leave you?

"Following a damn ghost," she muttered.

Exactly. So which would be worse?

She didn't want to think about it. She would just keep going, and not allow herself to be influenced either way.

The girl appeared at the top of an incline, looking over as if to check that Amanda was still coming, then she was gone once again.

With a sigh, Amanda started to mount the rise, planting her feet into the ground, and moving with her body slightly leaned forward to keep her balance.

17

On the ground, he sat by the fire, angled in such a way that she couldn't see him entirely. His mask was raised over his mouth, and she could hear the slurping sounds of his mouth as he dined on the chunk of meat he'd carved from her thigh. Only a partial section of his face could be seen from where she was, and it was hard to decipher from all the hair. It looked like a bush of brownish hair was stuck to his chin.

Whimpering, she glanced down at her wound—a black cavity, secreting blood. Her bottom lip began to tremble again, but she managed to get it pinned between her teeth.

She was going to try talking to him again. When she'd been hired at the hospital, they'd made her take a course on ways to properly handle yourself whenever one of the headcases from the loony ward broke out. There were countless methods they'd taught. But the one that stayed with her was trying to carry on a casual conversation with them. Supposedly, it distracted them so you could escape or confused them into thinking you were their friend.

She never believed it.

But she'd always been a good talker. Matt had always told her she could talk anyone down from a ledge.

He was good at that, filling her with such garbage that it made her blind to the person he truly was. Even the day she'd finally confronted him about the affairs she had solidly proved he was having. He'd tried to convince her he was a good guy, like what she'd learned in the class.

But she knew the truth. She'd gotten on the computer to check her email and found that, like an idiot, he'd forgotten to logout of Facebook. Not his regular account that she was a friend of, but the *secret* account that was just one of several with a different name and fabricated personality he had used to fuck multiple women, and even one man.

When she'd confronted him with the evidence, he'd made a face, and said, *You really think that's me?*

"Yes," she said, "I *know* it's you."

He'd denied it, but she wouldn't stop until he admitted it all. When he was finally the one talking, she realized she really hadn't wanted *all* the details. She got them anyway, and they'd haunted her ever since.

Disgusting smacks pulled her out of her painful reflections. She watched the man. He was licking off the blood that had dribbled onto his fingers from her cooked meat. When he finished, he adjusted the mask, so it was hiding all of his features once again.

Now or never.

"I know you can understand me."

He paused, slightly gazing back at her without turning his head all the way.

"Can you talk?"

He was immobile, like a piece of the woods that had sprouted from the ground.

"I bet you can. Want to talk to me?"

He turned his head forward. Now all she could see was the back of him, his shaggy hair and the entwined straps of the mask that was being devoured by the hair.

"Did I taste good? I sure smelled like I would. Is it like they say? Do humans taste like chicken?"

He stood up. Wiped his hands on his pants.

"What are you doing?"

He headed towards her. As he loomed closer, her breathing beefed up in speed. He removed the carving knife.

"No, please don't…"

So much for talking him into letting her go. She'd been reduced back to the sniveling little twerp she'd been the whole time.

He grabbed her tank top, yanking it down to expose her left breast. The shirt didn't rip, but it was now definitely stretched out. At first, she thought he was going to start fondling her. When he put the blade to her nipple, she quickly grasped that she was wrong.

Her words turned to squeals.

She felt the blade prick the soft tissue.

Then an explosion resounded around them. His head snapped back. He staggered away from Megan a couple steps. The tank top slipped from his fingers. It fell back on her breast, but hung loosely, barely covering her. Bringing his head back down, she saw that just above his left eye was a perfect dime-sized circle. Flaps of the mask fluttered in the breeze around the hole.

He stepped back two more steps, dropped down on his knees, then collapsed onto his side. The blood pooled in front of his face, mudding the dirt into a thick red paste.

Megan was on the verge of panic. She stared at the fallen psychotic, her breaths now high-pitched wheezes. She was trying to understand what just transpired.

She looked down at her breast. It was okay. Just a slight cut that blood was now oozing out of. Nothing major. Nowhere near as much as the amount coming out of the man's forehead.

He'd been shot.

It was just the two of them out here. How could he have been shot?

She recalled the loud bang. Definitely a gunshot.

How do you know? It's not like you hear them every day.

It was. She'd seen enough movies to know what they sounded like.

Okay. Then who was the triggerman?

"Allison," she gasped.

Could it be?

She turned her head as far to the right that she could. It was easy to spot the new arrival. And it wasn't her friend, posed with a hip cocked out and a gun aimed in front of her. But positioned behind a tree, a gun with a long barrel pointing to the spot where the psycho had just dropped was a scruffy man who might have been in his thirties. A thin runnel of smoke wafted out from the tip of the gun.

"You all right, girlie?"

Shocked, she slowly nodded.

"Looks to me like I got here just'n time."

Megan didn't respond, *couldn't* respond. She couldn't take her eyes off him.

Lowering the gun, he strutted into the clearing, nonchalantly approaching the fallen man. He nudged him with the toe of his boot. After a beat, he whistled.

"Deader than shit, and uglier than fuck." A strap dangled from the gun's barrel to the wooden stock of the other end. He threw it over his shoulder like a pocketbook strap. "What's going on, girlie?"

Her breathing still rapid, she managed to talk through wheezing huffs. "He killed my friends…Allison and Brian…"

Allison was dead, right?

"…and he came after me. I got lost in the woods, then Allison helped…" She looked at the man, saw his scruffy face scrunch with confusion, then decided to drop all references to Allison. "…I mean, he caught me, and brought me here. I don't know where I am. Please-please-please help me…"

She was about to continue but stopped when she saw him ogling her. He was shaking his head, but not like someone in disgust or pity, but more like someone who was surprisingly thunderstruck, as if he'd been given a gift he hadn't expected. His eyes glanced down to her chest three quick times.

"Wuh-what?" she asked.

"Well, this just beats it all." He looked away. "Rusty? Missy?"

There was some rustling in the woods, then two others even shabbier than this guy stepped out from behind the trees. A man and a woman, both young, both armed. The man was bald on top with a horseshoe of stringy hair touching his shoulders and held an ax. The girl was furnished with a double-barrel shotgun. Her hair pigtails, she was dressed like someone just off the train.

The entire hillbilly clan was smudged in filth.

"Whatcha got, Billy?" asked the girl, most likely Missy.

"A gift from the Lord, hisself. I told you if we kept workin' hard like we was, he'd bless us fer sure!"

The other guy, Rusty, beamed. From all the way over there, Megan could see his round eyes. "She's fer us?"

"She is now," answered Billy. He turned to Megan, winked. "One good deed deserves a reward."

"What the hell is this?" shouted Megan.

"A good day fors us, a shitty ones for you." He laughed.

Megan sobbed. What fight she had left had just been depleted.

Missy and Rusty entered the clearing. On their way past the man Missy asked, "Who's this?"

"Dead meat. I think he the one messin' around our plants."

"Don't look like the kind to be doing that," said Missy.

"How many other fuckers you reckon is this deep in the goddamn woods, other than us?"

She shrugged.

"I think I took care of our problem and gots a reward all'n the same day."

Rusty approached Megan, his goofy smile showing teeth pock-marked with cavities. "Can we keep her?"

"Just gotta get 'er down first."

"Stay the hell away from me," said Megan. "Just leave me here. Don't you dare fucking touch me!" Staying pinned to this damn tree was more appealing than going anywhere with this batch of hillbillies.

Billy talked to the others as if she weren't there. "Come help me find a hammer. Has to be around here somewhere."

"How you know that?" said Rusty.

"How else did those nails get 'n her arms you fuck-tard!?!"

The comment looked to have hurt Rusty's feelings.

Billy sighed. "Damn it, boy, I'm sorry. I didn't mean to hurt ya none."

"I'm all right."

"Good. Then get to looking. Help your sister look over there." He pointed by where the man lay.

Rusty seemed reluctant to go anywhere near the big man and Megan couldn't blame him for it. He went regardless of his feelings, probably because he feared Billy just as much.

They scoured the small area. It wasn't long before Missy gasped and grabbed the hammer off the ground near the fire pit. "Here it is, Billy!"

Billy smiled. "Good eyes, Missy. You always been able to find a brown kernel in shit anyways."

She smiled at that as if it had been the best compliment she'd ever received. She passed him the hammer.

Billy headed back over to Megan. She kicked a foot at him as he neared. Jumping back, he laughed. "Ooooweeee! She's a spirtfire if I ever seen one!"

Rusty laughed. "She sure is!"

All of them approached now, but it did nothing to deter Megan from throwing her legs up, trying to kick each of them.

She struck Missy in the gut, making her stumble back. Bent over, Missy shouted, "Damn bitch *kicked* me!"

"Rusty," called Billy. "Hold down a leg, and Missy you get the other one."

They pounced at once, not giving Megan a chance

to kick again. Hugging her legs, they forced them to the ground, and kept them grappled in place.

Megan cried out. Angered because of the defeat, and the desire of wanting to inflict at least a modicum of pain was going unfulfilled.

"Just hold 'er tight. I have a feelin' she's gonna try and run for it."

"Can't go far with this leg," said Rusty.

"Won't stop 'er from tryin'," said Billy.

And he was right. Even if both legs had been severed, she would still try and run.

He turned the hammer claw-end out. He ran it up her arm, clutching a nail in the arch between the two claws. After another wink, he pulled down. The nail wrenched out of the tree, tearing through her wrist and delivering another rush of pain down her arm. She cried out. It was unbelievable she could still feel this much pain. Shouldn't she be in shock by now? She wished for blank numbness to come soon.

Billy repeated the procedure with the other nail. It did not hurt as bad as the last. It was much, much worse. Her arms drooped by her side. She attempted a swing at Billy but couldn't lift her arm above her waist. It only dangled there like a useless appendage.

Billy laughed. "Need to hurry. She ain't got no feeling in her arm. Gotta move before she gets it back!"

He was wrong. She had plenty of feeling, all painful.

Quickly, he dislodged the remaining two nails in her other arm, blasting her arm with two arctic shots of pain. The arm dropped like a balloon that had just been popped. Now both arms swayed at her hips.

"All done. You're coming with us."

Missy released the one leg and was starting to stand when Rusty, noticing that Missy had done so, let the other leg go. The idea to retaliate had hardly registered in her mind when she rammed her shoulder into Billy's midsection. The force of the hit knocked Billy back.

Megan put her back against the tree for leverage and kicked Rusty on the chin. Then she threw up a knee, catching a distracted Missy on the cheek.

Megan moved in swift surprise, but she realized she had a problem when her momentum continued to carry over. She toppled over Missy's shoulders. Her back slammed the ground. She watched her stretched legs cut through the air as if she were doing a cartwheel. Her left leg crashed onto the ground first, the right landing on top of it.

Air shot out of her lungs. She couldn't breathe, and her butchered leg screamed. On her back, she stared up at a brilliant blue sky with fluffy white streaks. She wanted to lie there, enjoying the view and a few minutes of rest. She didn't have those minutes. She didn't even have seconds.

Megan needed to keep moving. Now, while they were down.

She rolled onto her stomach, pushing herself up with her hands. Her breast tumbled out of the stretched top. The slit nipple stung when air hit it. As she got to her knees, she stuffed her breast back behind the shirt.

Megan pushed her wild hair out of her eyes and checked on the hillbillies. Missy lay beside her, slightly stirring and groaning. Rusty was on his side watching her, his hand rubbing his chin with a grimace twisting his face. Then she looked over to where Billy should have been. She was prepared to find him holding his stomach, coughing as he tried to take in air.

His spot was vacant.

Where…?

She looked behind her and found him standing there. The hammer poised above his head.

"Damn…" she muttered.

The hammer came down.

18

Amanda gaped at the crude structure in revolted awe. A shelter of some kind erected with old tarp and camouflaged in leaves and sticks. It looked like it had been here for a very long time. How could something like this have existed without any of the rangers being cognizant of it?

She'd followed the girl to this spot. She was probably supposed to keep going, but after spotting this little shanty, Amanda had to stop and observe it. She could feel the sheer surprise on her face like an uncomfortable mask.

Gun drawn, she crept forward. She kept the pistol angled down and away, moving like a cop about to raid a meth lab. Approaching the shelter from the side, she noticed the tears, the destroyed rear wall. The gaping hole, and tattered pieces weaving in the gentle breeze.

"What the hell happened here?" she asked the trees around her.

She moved around to the backside, facing the giant gap, and peered inside. It was too dark to see anything. She shrugged the backpack off her shoulders, letting it fall to the ground. She unzipped the pack and rummaged around inside until feeling the cool metal surface of her Maglite. Then she tugged the light out of the bag, clicked it on, and aimed it into the black hole.

A runnel of light stabbed the darkness, the round disc illuminating the furnishings inside, a table cluttered in a wide assortment of objects, filthy laundry.

The light landed on someone.

A gasp of fright brushed the back of her throat. She staggered back a couple steps. "Who's in there?" She waited another moment then asked again. The silence in the air was thick and uncomfortable. After she still didn't gain a response, she moved back to the torn tarps with caution. The gun was ready to go bang if she needed it too.

She peered into the crudely made structure, the barrel of her gun aimed inside. She swept the light from wall to wall. The person still sat where she'd first spied them, slightly leaned forward, their yellow hair tangled and wild on their head.

"Ma'am? Are you okay?"

Amanda was about to go inside but noticed the woman's skin on her shoulders. It was the color of stained wood and horribly dried out. Amanda thought if she were to touch the skin it would feel like a leather jacket that had been in someone's attic for a decade.

A corpse.

Another dead body. Number three in the same day. But not the one she was looking for. Judging her looks, she'd been out here a long time.

After another swipe of the interior with her flashlight, Amanda decided it was the only body there to find. Everything else seemed deserted.

She wanted to do something about the lady inside, but there was nothing she really could do. She'd have to leave her behind, for now. When she decided to go back to the tower, she'd make sure to report it before they fired her.

A trickle of sweat slid down her cheek. She wiped it with the back of her hand. Even after the sweat was gone, she continued to rub her face, as if she might be able to wipe away the feel of the shelter.

Amanda sighed. She felt awful. This woman hadn't deserved whatever had been done to her. She wondered if the pot farmers had done this, too, or if she should start to suspect someone else was haunting these woods.

Haunting?

On that note, Amanda glanced over her shoulder to check the way ahead. She saw the dead girl waving her forward before trotting away, holding her head upright by the hair.

Amanda shuddered so hard she felt a cramp in her stomach. She thought she might have pulled a muscle.

I'm following a damn ghost.

Sounded crazy even in her mind but she believed it. A ghost was leading her to the missing girl. She felt an empty tug in her bowels, a twinge of dread.

Amanda quickly gathered her things, then got back to hiking.

19

Megan was aware of being on the ground. She could feel grits of dirt scraping against her face. Her skin itched from the grass and dried blood. Things scurried across her, ants probably, mosquitoes.

Sounding as if coming through a funnel, she could hear voices. Behind her somewhere, garbled and bendy. One voice stood above the others, demanding and barking orders.

Billy.

Now it was coming back in bits and she wished it would just stay forgotten. She wanted to go back to that blank state where she didn't know anything, where all she saw was black, in a deep sleep where she was oblivious to this madness. They could do whatever they wanted, so long as she didn't know what it was. So long as she didn't have to feel any of it.

She cracked her eyes open, just a feeble slit. Blurred,

she could see the woods: a haze of green and brown, smudged like a cheap painting.

There was movement within. As her vision became more focused, she realized the movement was actually Billy and Rusty walking around. Both had giant black trash bags thrown over their shoulders.

They dropped the bags just inches from Megan's head. Dirt puffed her face, flaking in her eyes. She blinked them out. A strong herbal scent wafted into her nose, bringing back her vigilance as if it were a smelling salt. It was a smell she recognized, and one she hadn't been able to enjoy since becoming an ER nurse three years ago.

She saw what had spilled out of the black trash bags was marijuana. Both bags were full of the freshly picked crop. The green arches seemed to twinkle in the sunlight.

Slowly raising her head, she winced, pain punching from the back of her skull. She reached behind her head, feeling a knot. When she brought her fingers back, they were wet with blood.

Another wound to add to the steadily growing list.

She groaned.

Carefully, she started to sit up when something suddenly stopped her. She felt a tug at her neck. Looking down at her chest, she noticed a chain trailing between her breasts, pulling the tank top taut against their mounds. She gripped it, running her fingers up the length to where the chain was wielded to an iron collar around her throat. She tugged at the iron choker, but it did no good.

"No need to try, hun," said Missy from behind her. "It ain't coming off. Not withouts tha' key."

Megan looked to her left and found Missy sitting on an overturned bucket. She was using a giant hunting knife to dig grime out from underneath her fingernails. She must have been sitting there the whole time she was out cold, keeping an eye on her.

Missy hardly looked concerned. "And," she added with a snicker, "I'm the one with the keys."

"Where am I?"

"Our spot."

Megan looked around, taking in the vicinity. She couldn't see much beyond where Billy and Rusty had gathered. Behind Missy was a large drum on a grate over some firewood. Tubes were attached to the top and trailed down the side into a giant witch's cauldron.

Megan understood what they were mixing in the pot and it wasn't witch's brew.

Moonshine.

This was their still.

"Shit," muttered Megan.

Missy giggled. "You lookin' at our still?"

Megan shook her head.

"Whatsa matter? 'Fraid we gonna kill ya since ya seen it?"

Megan didn't answer. She stared at the ground to avoid eye contact.

"We ain't gonna kill you cause of that. If'n you gots into our plants, then we'd kill you deader than a shit stain. But not cause of the still. Too many's doing the shine these days. Business is tougher than a two-dollar steak cooked burnt. But we number one in pot, yes'm, you better believe it." She fell quiet, her attention averted by her fingernails. She went back to picking at the pinky nail with the knife blade.

Megan looked Missy over. She had lemon-colored curls parted in pigtails. Big blue eyes, bright and full of dimwitted life. Her skin was tawny and smooth, with little smears of dirt here and there. She wore boots that looked so heavy Megan was surprised she could even lift her feet. Denim pants cut into briefs with the lower cambers of buttocks poking out from behind the frilly strings. She had a flannel shirt tied in front of a bra that struggled to hold back a pair of giant breasts.

Missy was almost beautiful. Compared to the guys, she was a super model.

"What do you want from me?" Megan asked.

Without looking up, "With you? That's easy. We wants to have some fun."

Megan practically scoffed, not surprised, and not really bothered.

Frowning, Missy leaned closer to Megan as if to study her. "This is whens they usually go all squally-like."

"What's the point?"

Missy looked at the sky as if the answer might be shaped in the clouds. Not finding it, she only shrugged. Then she went back to work on her nails, holding her hand out, with her fingers extended to survey them.

She made an approving face.

Megan looked down at the holes in her wrists. She was surprised they weren't bleeding any more than they had been. It was either a good sign or a really bad one. She didn't feel like she'd lost too much blood. They sure hurt, though. If she moved her hands a certain way, it felt like he was driving the nails in all over again. And they were also already becoming infected. Blackening around the inner layers of the hole, slips of green were scattered about. It needed to be washed out, and if she still had her bag, she could squirt giant dabs of disinfectant down in them. She didn't, so it hardly mattered.

Megan looked back at Missy. "So, did you know that guy?"

"Guy?"

"The one that hammered me to the tree!"

"Oh, him. No. I ain't never seen him before in my life. 'S funny, though. A man like that, you would think he'd be easy to spot out here, but I sure ain't never seen 'im."

Megan noticed Missy was gazing over her shoulder, so she glanced back and saw nothing of particular interest back there.

"I wonder who he was. Shame Billy gunned him down like that. Now we's won't never know." She puckered out her bottom lip. "I wonder if'n he one of those we heard about when we's was kids."

Finally, Missy had said something that intrigued Megan to hear more, and she wanted to kick herself for it. Too bad she couldn't. One leg had a slit calf, and the other had a chunk wedged out of its thigh. Now her wrists had a combination of four holes.

That are getting infected.

If she didn't get help for them soon, she would probably get blood poisoning thanks to the nails' tarnished metal.

It made the pain worse staring at her wrists, so she looked at Missy. She still had her bottom lip puckered out in a mock pout. Her cheeks were puffy and high on her face like a cherub.

"What'd you hear?" she asked the hillbilly girl.

Missy's face showed excitement as she leaned in close like she was about to share the utmost guarded secret of the backwoods. "When we's was little, there was'a this woman that lived way out yonder." She pointed behind her. "On the opposite side of the gorge, deep in the dark woods. You ever been out there before? The dark woods?"

"No."

"Ah, well, we used to camp out there with Ma and Papa when we's wuz little younglin's, and Papa would tell us this story of old Natalie Gunthrope. People believed she was'a witch."

Megan made a face.

"I know what you's a thinkin', and I can't blame you one for. But no, she wasn't all flyin' around on no damn broom, painting the moon in chicken's blood or nuthin' like that."

Megan felt the corners of her mouth being pulled

into a grin, and to her surprise she heard herself lightly chuckle.

Missy, proud of herself for getting a rise out of Megan, grinned right back. "When I was'a girl, I would lay in bed at night and be skeered to death that she would fly right by my winder. Swear to God-Almighty I was." Placing a hand over her heart, she pointed at the sky with her knife. "May He strike me dead if I'm lyin' to ya. Just go head."

Megan glanced up, silently hoping a single bolt of lightning would lash down from the sky and do just as Missy had dared, but no such luck. She must not have been lying.

"Anyways," continued Missy. "Papa said that she could do all kinds of curses and spells and magic stuff. The bad kind. Papa also said she was over a hun'red-years-old. You believe that shit? That's *old!*" She made a face as if old age was a disgusting disease.

"But how does that...that *psychopath* fit into that story?"

"I was get'n to that part, impatient ninny."

Megan almost laughed again but stopped herself before she could.

"People used to talk that she had a kid, a boy, a *real* ugly bastard too."

"Oh, shut up, Missy."

Billy.

"No one wants to hear that damn story," he said. "We heard it all the time when's we was kids."

Billy and Rusty were approaching from off to the

side. Megan watched them wearily, anticipating Billy would do something to hurt her.

Missy, angered she was interrupted, shot Billy with a nasty look. "We's was talkin' Billy. I don't care if'n you are my brother, I'll kick y'ass if you butt in again!"

Brother? These three are related?

Megan wanted to call bullshit because none of them looked even slightly similar. Their facial features were different. All of them seemed to have different eye colors. Their bodies were nowhere near identical. Billy was the tallest of the three, gangly with thin arms and giant hands. Rusty was slightly taller than Missy, and a foot shorter than Billy. And, other than Missy, this was a trio of the ugliest assholes this side of inbred mountain.

Billy had a grossed-out look on his face. "And don't talk to her, either. The way you's two was goin' on I thought you might start all lezzin' out on us. Give me and Rusty a *real* good show!"

Rusty grimaced. "Ewww, gross."

Billy looked at Missy, mocking anger now. "See what ya done? And you know how poor ol' Rusty only likes the cornholes!"

Missy and Billy laughed. Megan was not amused. She felt her stomach twist.

"I do not," argued Rusty. "I just don't like the two girls crap. It ain't right!"

"*You* ain't right," said Billy.

Missy intervened before her brothers' argument could escalate into something out of hand. "Come on,

Billy, lemme finish the story!"

"No. You tellin' it all stupid, anyway."

"Then you tells her!"

Billy eyed Megan suspiciously. "Nah. She duhn't want to hear it none no-how."

Missy gawked at Megan in pleading agony. For whatever reason she couldn't understand, she felt bad for the hillbilly girl. Something about her just oozed sweetness. Maybe it was the fact that she was a brainless twit, so stupid that she was cute.

Megan sighed. "I do. I want to hear the story."

Billy leaned down, putting his scruffy face right at hers. "You sure? Ain't bullshittin' just to get Missy all giddy?"

She heard Missy squeal as if she'd heard something to make her blush. Megan slowly shook her head.

Billy straightened, adjusted his belt. "Well a'ight. Billy Judd here will tell ya the story to knock ya socks off!"

"Billy who?" asked Megan. She needed to clarify she'd heard him correctly.

"Billy Judd."

"Judd?"

"Yeah." He shared a look with Rusty and Missy that suggested Megan's ignorance.

"You three...are the Judds?"

"So what if'n we are? Have you heard of us or something?"

She'd heard of the Judds all right, just not this trio. "No."

"Ya gonna shut your trap so I can tell the story or not?"

"I'm shutting my trap."

"A'ight then." He cleared his throat. "Missy already told'ya 'bout how they sez that the old hag was a witch. And she was. And, Zeb, her son, was a monster. They says she was impreg-er-nated by the devil hisself 'cause wuh'nt any man out there that'd fuck her. Except fer Rusty and he wuhn't born yet."

Billy and Missy laughed at Rusty's expense. Rusty, the punchline, only shrugged.

Wiping a tear from his eyes, Billy continued. "Anyhoo, she birthed this devil kid. Now he's grown, and they says he runs through the woods like a demon, killin' anyone and anything that gets in his way."

Megan looked at them with an expression of skepticism adorning her face. But she couldn't help the notion creeping up in her mind that she had been nearly killed more than once by that very devil kid. She shook her head to jar that idea free. "Come on. You don't believe that, do you?"

Rusty slapped his legs. "Hell yeah we does!"

Billy said, "Kids been'a disapurring all over fer years. We's had friends when we was little go up missin'. They say it was ol' Zeb. He can move through the trees as if'n he waren't there a'tall. Like a…a…" His face scowled with frustration at not finding the word.

"A ghost?" offered Megan.

"Damn right, a ghost!"

"You saw him," said Missy. "Wasn't he a monster?

A *real* mean bastard?"

Yes, I saw him. Felt his wrath, too.

She couldn't believe herself. What was she thinking? Letting their dumb backwoods story spook her. She felt foolish and more than a little naïve. "He wasn't a damn demon combing the woods. Just some sick psychopath that butchered my friends! He's not some force of nature sent up here from the bowels of hell. Just a man! A fucked-up man!"

She burst into tears. She attempted to shield her face with her hands but moving them sent spears of pain through her in hot flashes.

The Judds watched her sob, shocked and uncomfortable.

It was Billy who spoke first. "Stop that mess."

She nodded but didn't stop.

"I said *stop*!"

Megan sucked in her snuffles, her lip flapping uncontrollably. "Suh-sorry." She backhanded her eyes, keeping her wounds away from the salty tears.

"It's okay," said Missy.

"No, it's not," said Billy. "All whiny and shit."

"Her friends was killed!"

"Big deal!"

"Billy Jean Judd, you should be ashamed of yourself."

Billy slapped his hands to his hips, fuming. Hot gusts of air spurted from his nostrils. "Why we even wasting so much goddamn time talkin' bullshit wit' her anyhow?"

"Because I like her," answered Missy. "She's nice. Not the fake nice the others likes to be, neither. The real nice. That's why."

"Oh, shut your face lemonhead!"

"Don't talk to her like that!" Megan slapped her hand to her mouth, flinching against the pain it caused in her wrist. She couldn't believe those words had come out of her mouth.

Billy quickly raised his hand to her. Megan braced herself for the smack, expecting it to come any moment.

"That'sa good way to talk to the man that saved yer life!"

Megan lowered her hand from her mouth. "Saved my life…? Really?" She laughed, surprising herself just as much as the Judds. *Judds.* Her laugh turned to a maniacal guffaw, loud and rampant. Wild-eyed, wicked smile, her sanity had to be questioned by the very sound of it.

Rusty scratched his slick dome. "Why's she laughing, Billy?"

"I don't know." He turned to Megan. "What's got you so tickled?"

His question only brought more laughter. She waved a hand at him, hoping he understood she was asking him to give her a minute to compose herself.

She could see the rage making his skin bubble. "You think I'm funny?"

Gripping the chain, he jerked it back, choking her. Her laughter snagged. Eyes bulging, now she retched, her air cut short.

Clapping, Rusty laughed and cheered his brother. Missy stood, ran over to Billy, and placed a hand delicately on his shoulder.

"Don't be mean to her, Billy!"

"I done told ya once to shut up!"

"If you don't stop, you'll kill 'er! And if you's kill 'er, we won't get to have our fun with 'er." Her hand ran down his chest, making its way to his crotch.

"Get your damn hand off my pecker! I ain't in no mood for that kinda fun with her. Not no more!"

He let go of the chain. Megan fell onto her side, grasping at her choker, asthmatically sucking in air. It just wouldn't come fast enough. She worried he'd damaged something in her throat, and she wouldn't be able to get the air she needed and would slowly choke to death right here on the ground. Surrounded by three hicks watching her with dumbstruck expressions on their stupid faces.

Except for Missy, she figured she would probably be upset. She might even cry.

Then she noticed she could breathe a little better. Still not how she wanted, but it was definitely coming easier now.

Billy backhanded the spittle from his mouth. A coy smile formed. "I just want to make her scream...and bleed."

"That's fun too," said Rusty. "I like that!"

"I know you do, you fuckin' sicko!"

Rusty lowered his head, ashamed. Then he nodded

in agreement.

Missy looked panicked. "Whatcha gonna do to her?"

"Little bit of this, lots of that."

"Tell me!"

"What's it matter?"

"Just curious is all."

Billy smirked. "Uh-huh, sure you are. If'n you must know. I planz to cuts her up real good. Gonna break out Esther."

Rusty howled. "Esther? Holy shit!"

Megan, hand clutched to her throat, listened attentively. She wondered who Esther was. Another family member? Just like in the movies, this one would be the sibling they kept hidden from the rest of the world because they were so hideously mutated with an unquenchable thirst for human blood.

Or it could be a dog. That seemed more likely. A dog trained to eat flesh.

Missy looked confused. "I thought Esther was broked."

Broked?

What did she mean by that?

"She was. Not no more, though. I fixed her up *real* good."

Missy stepped back, suddenly nervous.

"Stay with her, Missy, and don't you dare do nuthin' stupid, hear?"

Missy nodded, a pout on her face.

Rusty came up beside Billy, an eager grin splitting

his face. "Let's go get the stuff, Billy!"

"We are in a second." He looked at his sister sympathetically. "Hell, Missy, you like this 'un, huh?"

Missy nodded. "Yes, I do, Billy, lots."

Billy sighed. His mouth strained to a thin, tight line.

Megan almost smiled because the sulking was working.

"A'ight. I guess'a you can fondle her up while we're gone. Get in all your kicks 'cause she's gonna be screaming when we's get back."

Excited, Missy turned to him, putting her hands on his chest. "You mean it?"

"Yeah, go head. We'll take our time getting Esther, so you can have all yer fun."

Clapping, Missy hopped up and down, her breasts bouncing behind her shirt, pigtails flapping at the air around her.

Billy smiled like a proud parent, then turned around. He put his arm around Rusty. "Let's go. Let 'em have their fun."

Megan noticed a look on Rusty, one that showed regret. It wasn't an expression of envy, but one that she read as pity. He felt sorry for her? If that was the case, what in the hell kind of 'fun' would Missy be inflicting?

She watched them vanish in the woods, then looked up to where Missy stood over her.

Her eyes were hungry and full of lust.

20

Megan steeled herself, swallowed the lump in her throat. It felt as if it might strangle her, as if a wad of wool were lodged in there. She studied Missy.

"I didn't think theys was ever gonna leave!" Missy ran a finger down Megan's cheek. "Yer so purty, you know that?"

"Um…"

"I bet folks tells you that all the time, don't theys?"

Missy got down on her knees between the V of Megan's legs. She rubbed a hand up Megan's arm, sprouting up ridges of gooseflesh. Smiling, her hand moved to Megan's shoulder, lightly squeezing. "You're skin's so soft." She ran her tongue across her lips.

Megan tried to remain calm. "Missy." Fingertips brushed her neck. She shivered. "Missy. You have to let me go."

"I don't wanna." Her focus was on Megan's body,

savoring her.

"You *have* to. You heard what Billy said. He's going to kill me. If that happens, all the fun is gone. We can never have fun again."

"I get my fun in right now, and you's ruinin' it with all your squawkin'. Now shut up and let me play whiles I can!" Missy glided her finger down Megan's arm to the holes in her wrist left by the nails. She traced the coarse ridges with a fingertip. "Whoa, it goes all the way through. They hurt?"

Megan was on the verge of shouting but contained it. "Yes, they hurt. A lot. Let me go. Better yet, come with me. We can get out of here, together, and think about all the fun you can have then."

Missy pursed her lips. "Won't be the same." She tickled Megan's skin.

Megan tried to ignore how good it felt being touched the way Missy was doing it. Delicately. Treating her with tender wonderment and admiration. She kind of liked it. "Yes, it will. It'll be *better.*"

"Naw, it won't."

"Don't you want to get away from here? Aren't you tired of living in the woods? *Please* let me take you out of here. Just show me the way out, and I'll take you with me."

Missy shushed her. She used her other hand to rub Megan's cheek. "You's crazy as hell, you know that? We don't live in the woods. We gots a house back near Cripple Creek. We jus' camp out here a couple nights a month ta check on the crop, that's all. And I know what you're thinkin'. It ain't no damn shack or nuthin' where we has to shit in da woods or nuthin'. We gots power, a TV, and even the damn intranet."

Megan stuttered, so much she wanted to say, but she was unable to get the words organized. She'd simply assumed the Judds were mountain people that lived in a shack much like the one Allison—or who she thought was Allison—had led her to. They weren't backwoods hicks but hi-tech hillbillies. She'd completely misjudged them and felt like an idiot now for labeling them like what she saw in movies.

Megan bellowed out in horror when she felt Missy's finger push into one of the wounds on her wrist. She felt it squirming in the hole, sloshing around. Fingering it.

Missy's eyes had rolled back in her head, her mouth slightly parted. And she was cooing like an infant, sighing as if this was orgasmic to her.

Then she plopped the finger out. The tip was blotted in blood. She raised her trembling hand to Megan's right breast and drew a smudgy heart. "I love you…"

Megan's wrist felt as if it had been held against a burner, searing with hot pain. "If you love me…you'll help me get out of here." She had started crying and was appalled she sounded so pathetic. But it was all she had left. Her courage was gone, her strength, willpower. She had nothing.

So, she didn't resist when Missy made her lie on her back. Didn't put up a fight when Missy ripped her already stretched tank top down the middle with a vicious swipe, exposing her breasts. And she didn't even care when Missy tore a giant hole in her shorts at the crotch.

Almost, she *almost* did something when Missy put her tongue inside her, but the resolution hastily passed. Then Missy slipped two fingers in, and it kind of hurt, but once she relaxed her hips it didn't feel so bad.

Missy continually shoved her fingers in and out as her tongue flicked and licked.

Finally, she pulled her mouth away from Megan's sex, climbed on top of her and started kissing her with lips glazed in Megan's juices. Her tongue shoved its way into Megan's mouth.

"Grab my ass," Missy demanded.

Megan obliged. Missy gasped into her mouth as she struggled to free herself of the flannel shirt. It hurt having even someone as small as Missy squirm around on top of her. Her whole body was a canvas of aches and bruises and abrasions.

Missy chucked her shirt away, then sat up, straddling Megan's lap. She reached behind her back, unhinged the bra, and let it drop. Her heavy breasts sagged only a little. She had a lovely pair that any girl would be envious of—pleasantly shaped with small, pinkish nipples that stood erect to little points.

"Grab them," she told Megan.

Megan reached up with both hands. Her left wrist was bleeding thanks to Missy's exploring finger. She cupped a breast with each hand, smearing blood on one of them.

Missy moaned. "Now, pinch my nipples, hard as you can."

Megan took one between each thumb and forefinger, then tweaked them with all she could muster.

Missy leaned her head back and moaned a throaty gasp. "You're so good…so damn good!"

Megan enjoyed the pinching. It was nice to be inflicting some kind of pain on someone else, even if the person receiving it was enjoying it immensely.

Missy tore away from Megan so suddenly that she gasped. Standing up, Missy shoved her shorts down her legs. She had some trouble getting them to move over her boots. Eventually she succeeded.

"Like what ya see?" She put her hands on her hips, modeling for Megan. "No hair."

Hairless from the shoulders down, the band of skin between her thighs much paler than the rest. She'd recently shaved. The sun caught little spikes of downy hair just starting to sprout.

"It's…nice," gulped Megan.

Missy turned from side to side, then slowly spun a circle to exhibit her bare rump, a dimple at each buttock. She faced frontward again.

She got back on the ground, lying on her side against Megan. She felt the hillbilly girl's breasts squishing against her arm. Missy gripped a handful of Megan's hair and made her sit up, then she spread her legs, putting one on each side of Megan.

"It's my turn," she said in a whispery voice.

Megan understood what she meant even before Missy shoved her face against her wet, hairless chasm.

21

Rusty wished the girls weren't being so loud. The screams weren't that bad. He kind of enjoyed hearing those, but the sex sounds were just too much. Those were gross, the wet smacking sounds, and the grunts. He couldn't stop the soured look forming on his face.

Billy laughed. "Boy, Missy sure knows how to gets 'em all gaspy don't she?"

Rusty could see his brother was hard. "Yeah. She gets really weird sometimes."

"Hey, shut up, she's our sister."

"Well, that don't mean she don't get weird. I thinks she likes tha' girls more than the boys."

"Who cares if she does?"

"It ain't right."

"Oh, get off it. You like the boys better than the girls and *that* ain't right. I can understand if'n a girl just wants to have her another girl. I gets that, but two dudes?" He shook his head, making an expression very similar to Rusty's own. "I don't see's why you like the butt stuff."

"That's a lie!" He *did* like the boys. He liked the way they felt on the inside. Not all slippery how girls liked to get. A man's ass just seemed to be made for a pecker.

"You're right, though," said Billy. "She's a fuckin' loon!"

They had entered their camp, passing their sleeping bags spread out through the small area. Rusty stopped by the spent campfire. He'd probably be the one they sent to fetch fresh wood for tonight's fire. It was always him.

Billy kept walking to the large duffel bag they kept the tools in. Squatting beside it, he untethered the head, and reached inside. There were clattering sounds as he removed the gardening tools.

It always got like this when it came to Esther. There was a hype to her that Billy liked to drag out for as long as possible, building her up. It wouldn't last very long today, though, especially since that girl had really gotten Billy's dander up. He was already drooling thick foamy strings while he wrenched Esther out from the sack and sat her on the ground as if displaying her.

She had a small yellow body, and a long blade with a chain of teeth layered around it. A chainsaw. Nothing more. Rusted in spots, stained in various places, she was a well-built machine that Billy gaped at like a teenage boy peeping through the window of a high school senior girl undressing. Drool spattered her metallic body.

"Billy? You a'ight?"

"Fine. Just fine."

Rusty shook his head, then looked toward the woods. He saw a flicker of movement. Something snapped. The branches jiggled. "Hey, Billy?"

"What Rusty?"

"You ever get the feelin' you's bein' watched?"

Billy looked up. "Watched?"

"Yeah. I can't shake it. Been feelin' like someone's watchin' us since we gots back here."

"Who th'fuck would be watchin' us?"

Rusty had an idea but he didn't want to say. Hearing Billy retell that story about Zeb the Witch Boy, and Missy thinking he was the guy Billy had shot, made him think *he* was the one doing the watching. He wouldn't admit it to Billy, though. Not unless he wanted to be hacked on.

Billy could have read his mind. "You gettin' all jumpy 'cause a that guy I shot down, ain't ya?"

"Why's would I be bothered over a dead man?"

"The way you act'n, boy. You act'n like somebody walked over your grave."

"You sure he was dead?"

"Hell yeah I'm sure! How many men you know can take a slug in the skull and still be livin' to talks it over?"

"None folks, I guess…"

"You got'damn right, none folks, that's who."

Rusty smiled. "Lessin' he's the son of a witch."

Billy glanced up at the sky as if to ask the Lord "why

him?" Then he looked at Rusty. "You's kiddin' me, right?"

Rusty shrugged.

"Boy, I oughtta wear out three sets of kneecaps kickin' your ass! They's ain't no damn witch boy runnin' around these woods. I done tolt ya."

"Ain't what I heardt. I heardt they's one."

"Who told ya that shit?"

Rusty shrugged. He couldn't recall who had, or honestly, *if* anyone had.

"You 'bout dumber than shit on a cone. We's been comin' out to these'a here mountains since we was kids, and we ain't never saw nothin'."

"Yeah we have!"

Billy scowled.

"Remember?"

"I don't 'member shit!"

Rusty knew he was lying. "We saw somethin' one time."

"Probably your pecker shot some weenie snot in yer eye and you thought it was a ghost!" He shook his head as if Rusty was an imbecile. "I'm done havin' this talk witcha, boy." He looked away from Rusty, still crouched over the bag.

Sighing, Rusty looked where the noise had registered from.

Neither of them noticed someone approaching, the craggy boots, and tattered pants hanging in streams above the laces.

"And besides," added Billy, "if'n he was here, I'd

just have to pop him again."

Rusty turned just in time to witness Billy's head being lopped off in one quick swipe. A glimmer from a giant blade flashed harsh light into his eyes. The head landed on the ground a few away with a moist *thunk.*

The stump of neck spurted blood like a red fountain.

Rusty Judd opened his mouth, silently screaming as no sounds came out. He cupped his hands over his mouth like a frightened little child. He felt like a child right now. All he wanted to do was curl up in a ball and cry. He was looking at a dead person, the guy they'd left behind. The man was moving about just fine despite Billy's declarations. His mask was blotted red in a spread pattern from the bullet wound. He slid the machete back into its sheath.

He hardly gave Rusty two glances as he reached down and lifted Esther off the ground. Billy's headless body dropped forward, landing on the sack. Blood jettisoned from two holes in the neck.

Rusty's legs betrayed him and gave out. He dropped down on his knees. His eyes fixed on the walking dead person.

The man gripped the pulley-handle, then jerked it back. The saw reeled to life, puttering puffs of yellowish smoke, contaminating the air with the gag-inducing odor of gas and oil. He turned around to face Rusty. He was a giant man, with shoulders like a wall. He pulled back on the throttle a few times, really making Esther roar. Billy had never gotten that kind of response from her. This guy really knew how to handle a weapon.

He advanced towards Rusty, closing the short distance between them. He raised the saw high in the air. The sun was behind him, outlining him in golden hues that gleamed off the colossal piece of equipment like a swirling bar against the brilliant blue of the sky.

Rusty shrieked now. The spinning chain came down on the top of his bald head. His body quaked as the grinding teeth chopped through his skull. It didn't stop until it had gone all the way through him, splitting his body into two, equally halved Rustys.

22

Missy gripped Megan's head with both hands, mashing her lips against her groin. She ground her hips ardently against Megan's face, smearing her juices over her nose, into her eyebrows, and dousing her chin.

The sudden rumble of a tiny engine made them both jump.

Missy shoved Megan away as she sat up with a start. "What was that?"

Megan wiped her mouth. The back of her hand was smeared in clear streaks. She looked at Missy, whose attention was diverted towards the noise.

"Sounds like they got Esther goin'." She turned back, worried. "We gots to hurry. They's comin'. And I haven't gotten to yet."

Grimacing at the wet stripes on her hand, she glanced over to her side. Her eyebrows arched.

It was just sitting there as if Missy had forgotten all

about it. She looked at the hillbilly bombshell, saw her attention was still diverted, and reached for the object. There was a trembling wave of satisfaction when her fingers curled around the hilt.

"Guess we better hurry up," said Missy. "They's gonna be heres any minute." Missy crawled back to Megan who had an arm hidden behind her back. "I's so close, too. Shouldn't take but a minute…"

Missy leaned over, putting a hand on each of Megan's shoulders. She kissed Megan on the side of her neck, then put her lips right at her ear. "It'll all be over soon. I promise."

"It already is."

"Wha…?"

Missy's voice was cut off by a wet punching sound. Blood sprayed out of her mouth. Megan felt it spatter her ear and cheek. Missy made gargling sounds as Megan twisted the blade of Missy's knife in her stomach.

"I'm sorry," Megan said.

Missy jerked against her. Megan continued holding her, preventing her from pulling away. Missy's arms squeezed tighter as Megan shoved the knife even deeper.

Missy moaned. Megan could feel the blood exuding from her mouth on her neck. The blood coming from her stomach had doused her hand like a warm liquid glove. It was hot as soup and thick like cough syrup.

"What…d'you…do to me?"

"I'm sorry," she said again.

Missy's burden shifted when her legs gave out. Megan scurried back and let her fall. She landed beside Megan's legs, rolled over, and glared up at her with enlarged eyes full of shock. Trails of blood sketched down her face and ran into her hair. The lemony locks were becoming sticky clumps.

The knife's handle jutted up from her stomach like a lever. Missy twitched a few more times before finally going still. She stopped breathing. The surprised reaction of betrayal had frozen on her face. Her eyes continued to glower, humiliated and heartbroken. A tear trickled down from each one.

Megan's words flew out of her in a single gust:

"I'msorryifyouwould'vejustshownmehowtogetoutI wouldhavetakenyouwithme!"

She cried body-quaking sobs. She turned away from Missy, unable to look at her anymore. Then she spotted Missy's shorts crumpled into a ball of fringy denim on the ground.

The keys!

Her eyes widened, hope building. She crawled toward them in a frantic dash. When she had almost reached the shorts, the chain snapped her right back. She landed on her buttocks, coughing. Not bothering to catch her breath, she quickly tried reaching for them again.

The shorts were no more than an inch out of reach. She strived to reach them, her arm extended as she madly groped. She wished her fingers would suddenly grow enough so she could snatch the shorts.

That buzzing sound was growing louder. She'd almost tuned it out entirely during the melee with Missy, but now it was impossible to ignore. Not only was it louder, but progressively rising in volume.

Coming closer.

The stout tang of gasoline wafted through the air. It reminded her of being twelve and riding on the back of her brother's dirt bike. Being on the back, it was all she could smell the whole ride. The memory almost made her cry.

When the psychopath revealed himself, injured but vigilant, revving the tiny motor as hard as it could handle, she did.

He looked at Missy leaning against the tree, then brought his eyes back to Megan. The steady buzz was hell to her ears, her brain vibrated in her skull.

The motor was killed, sputtering down to a stop. Silence tinkled back from the earsplitting ruckus of the saw. He sat it down by his feet.

Megan assumed that was Esther. She wasn't surprised Billy had given a name suited for a grandmother to a power tool.

The man, keeping his eyes on Megan, reached behind his back. He slowly withdrew one of the two-bladed axes. Lowering it, the blade dangled by his ankle.

So this was it. All the fighting, the running, letting a crazed hillbilly sexpot do things to her in hopes that she could catch her off guard and escape. All of it was for naught. Had she known this was how it would end, she wouldn't have bothered.

Maybe it was better this way. She definitely didn't have the stamina to fight anymore. She was just so tired.

"Okay," she said. "Do it."

He raised the ax above his head. Closing her eyes, she braced herself for the impact of the hefty blade. The final blow. She hoped it would be quick. One brunt slam, then she would feel nothing else.

A rustle of movement. The whoosh of the ax cutting air.

Then the clank of the chain snapping. She felt vibrations travel through the collar.

There was no additional pain.

She cracked one eye open, checking. The other slowly opened next. He stood before her in his signature stance.

Looking down, she checked the chain. It was broken. Before the thought that she could run had even registered, he'd already reached down and grabbed the section hanging from the collar. He wrapped it around his hand a couple times. Then he stood up straight, returning the ax to the holder behind his back.

Megan had no desire to make for a run. There really was no point. He'd just snatch the chain back, hurting her throat even more than it already was.

He tugged on the chain a couple times, signaling it was time to go. Sighing, Megan stood up. She crossed her arms across her breasts. She wished she could do something about the tattered hole in her shorts, but it would have to be left the way it was.

She noticed Billy's rifle leaning against a tree several feet away. She'd love to get her hands on the gun, but it was way out of reach. Might as well have been on another planet.

She glanced at Missy. And gasped.

The knife. It was right there. She could easily grab it, but he would notice her reaching over and yanking it out of Missy's stomach.

He got to walking.

Now!

Megan faked a stumble and dropped on top of Missy. Her hand gripped the handle of the knife and quickly pulled it out. It made a sloshing sound as it was extracted, like cutting watermelon. Before he could turn to see what the commotion was, she tucked the knife against her stomach, then hugged herself like she was hurting. She made sure the blade was flat against her skin. It felt cold and sticky.

He stopped, turned back, and stared at her a moment. Although she couldn't see his face, she could tell his suspecting gears were turning. He walked towards her. Megan sat up, blocking Missy from his view. For a horrifying moment, Megan thought he'd seen the knife and would come take it from her. He didn't. He kept walking right past her until the chain had almost run out of slack. Then he whipped the chain, sending a wave up the length. It popped her in the neck. Her head rocked to the side, almost pulling her body with it. She managed to stay squatted, thankfully, because if she'd had fallen back the knife would have been uncovered. It might have even slammed into her.

That would have been a way to go.

Her skin stung where the chain had smacked it. He lifted his hand, preparing to repeat the punishment, so she quickly got up. She understood he was going to take the rear to keep his eyes on her.

She got going and he followed, guiding her along like a dog on a leash.

23

Amanda didn't see the girl. She'd been waiting by a tree but when Amanda got near, she'd run off. This had been the simulation for the last long while. So, Amanda was surprised when she looked around the tree and didn't find her running ahead, showing her which way to take next.

"Where'd you go?" she muttered.

From where she stood, she made a slow circle. She saw no trace of the girl, nor did she find any indication of where she might have gone.

Now Amanda wondered if she'd ever been there at all.

Of course not.

Amanda had convinced herself she was being led to somewhere important by the ghost of the dead girl, and as crazy as that was, she hadn't been bothered by it. Somehow, it felt right, like this was how it was supposed to be. So, she'd gone along with it, not questioning the foolishness of it all.

When the chomp of approaching footsteps caught her attention, she knew she'd been brought here for a reason. She spun around, pressing against the tree. Her breasts were squished against the bark, and it hurt when the little jagged tips poked her through her tank top.

She peered around the side, only exposing herself from the eyes up.

"Holy shit."

Several feet ahead she saw a giant beastly man walking a young woman like a canine. She knew right away this was the girl she'd been looking for. It was hard to see them clearly through the dense tree population. But from what she could tell, the guy was wearing a mask. The girl was naked, or close to it.

She raised her gun, switching the safety to off. There was no shot to take. With all the trees, their limbs, there was way too much interference. She lowered her gun, waiting for them to get out of sight, then snuck out from behind the tree and followed them.

24

An hour of walking and they were back at the clearing, the bodies, the tree she had been hammered to. Nothing had changed since Megan was last here.

She glanced over to the girl displayed on the other tree. She wondered how close *she'd* come to getting away. Was her hope extended and snatched right back like Megan's had been?

She felt the choker pull at her throat with some force. It was the way someone would tug at the reigns strapped to a horse. Then it was yanked to the side, and so was she. He was making her turn, and she knew where he wanted her to go.

Back to the tree.

Megan slipped the knife into the front of her shorts, praying the blade wouldn't lick her where Missy had been. She moved with the swift current of the chain, stumbling over loose sticks and pinecones. If she couldn't keep up, she would fall, break her neck.

Maybe I should.

She wondered how bad it would hurt. Would it be quick and painless, or slow and agonizing? Just let the weight go to her knees and she'd find out.

She couldn't do it. Even though the next several hours, days, or even weeks would be more agony than she could possibly imagine, she wouldn't take her own life.

Megan felt the chain going to the right. He took her back to the tree where she had been nailed, then looped the chain around it a couple times.

He left some slack, but not much, just enough that she could move her head, but there wasn't much else. She kept her hand over the hole at the crotch of her shorts to keep him from seeing the knife blade. She was tempted to use it now, but she knew if she did, she might only get one slash at him. She needed a lot more than that. She'd hold off, for now.

He turned away from her, moving toward the iron pan sitting on top of the grate. The fire was quenched, having burned itself out while they were away. He removed the machete from his hip, examining the blade.

"Why haven't you killed me?"

He looked at her.

"I don't understand. Why don't you just finish me off? God knows you want to." She shrugged. "I mean—you tried to kill me and when you had me earlier, you didn't do it, and then back there you could have killed me again. You'd won, but you didn't." Whine was returning to her voice, she fought to detain it. "Why? Just tell me what I'm here for. Why?"

He took a deep breath, his shoulders rose and fell. His eyes were transfixed on her. He raised his empty hand as if he was about to answer.

"Freeze!"

Megan jumped at the abrupt boom of a voice. She looked to her right, and saw a woman marching out from the woods in a rigid stance, a pistol leveled at the man's chest. She wore khaki shorts that hugged her hips and a white tank top. There was another shirt tied around her waist, and she could see the golden points of a badge pinned to the front as it flapped against her thigh.

She recognized her from yesterday morning. The forest ranger operating the desk at the station they'd signed in at.

The man turned his gaze from Megan back to the ranger, then back to Megan. It appeared he was trying to decide who he wanted.

"Drop the machete! *Now!*"

He did one more back and forth glance, then released his grip on the machete. It fell, penetrating the earth blade down.

The ranger gave Megan a cautionary glance. "Ma'am? Are you all right?"

Megan laughed. She hadn't meant to. It just came out, a shrill cackle. "Not at all."

The man twitched, bringing the ranger's attention

back to him. "Get BACK!" She hadn't relinquished her guard. Aiming the gun squarely at his chest, she was ready to fire.

He didn't move, only continued to stand there as if sculpted from concrete.

The ranger spoke to Megan. "Can you free yourself?"

Although she already knew she couldn't, Megan reached for the collar and gave it a couple tugs. "No...I can't...I can't..."

"It's okay. I'll take care of it."

Keeping her gun pointed at the man, she walked over to Megan, sweeping her head from side to side. Probably looking for others who might be hiding within the trees.

"There isn't anyone else out here."

"He's alone?'

"As far as I know. There were some others, but he killed them too."

"Others?"

"Yeah, hillbillies. Shiners with some pot plants somewhere around here."

The ranger stopped. "Pot plants?"

"Yeah, they had bags of the stuff. Why?"

Megan thought she saw the hints of a smile on the ranger's face. "No reason." She looked where the chain was looped. "I'm going to need you to help me slacken it some. Arch your feet, push up on your toes."

"Oh—okay." Megan didn't know if she could. Her calf was hurt, her thigh was hurt, she doubted she had the strength to do it. To her astonishment, she found she was able to lift herself quite efficiently.

The ranger tugged at the chain, peeling it around the tree, then she dropped the tip down through the loop. All the tension was removed.

Megan fell back against the tree, breathing much easier.

"Better?" asked the ranger.

Megan was about to answer and tell her just how much better it was, but her words turned to a snagged gasp when the blade of a knife burst through the ranger's forearm, the gun soaring.

Screaming in shock, she held her arm. The pain looked prominent, but it appeared the surprise was even more so.

Where'd he get the knife!?

He probably had dozens of them hidden all over his body. Stupid.

We were so stupid to think he wouldn't have more.

Megan saw he was already approaching, his machete brandished with a clump of dirt attached to the tip of the blade.

He gripped the ranger by the back of the neck in the same fashion he had with Allison. He raised her off the ground. She swatted, punched, and slapped at him to no avail. Her feet kicked off the ground, coming close to his knees but not connecting.

The man studied her in a disturbing admiration. Mesmerized. He could see something inside of her. Something he wanted.

He let her go. She hit the ground, landing hard on her rump. She gaped up at him, huffing. Her hair had fallen out of the tie, strands of it dipping into her face.

The man grinded his hand around the machete's handle, looking the ranger over. Then he turned to the tree Megan had occupied.

It was vacant.

And the blade of Missy's knife punched through the front of his throat.

25

Amanda shrieked when a knife's blade ripped through his neck, just under his Adam's apple. He cupped a hand to his throat, stumbling sideways. He looked back.

Blood spurted from the man's throat, splashing Amanda in a crimson facial. She held up her arms to cover the raining blood. Turning her head away from her shield of arms, she spotted the girl—crouched down, ruffling her hands through the grass.

They came back with a hammer.

Feral-like, she screamed and lunged for the masked man.

One whack to the head, he whipped and spat blood through the dangling flap of the mask. The girl jumped, bringing the hammer down on top of his head. Then she swung it from one side, and the other, and back again. She continued to do this, growling in raging approval whenever the hammer connected with his head.

Finally, he dropped down to a knee. She struck him again. He shoved her back. She landed on her rump, momentarily derailed, but was quick to get back up and rush him again.

Amanda couldn't take this anymore, not even a man like him deserved what the girl was doing to him. "Stop!"

If the girl had heard the order, she wasn't giving any indication to it. She swung the hammer again. It caught him on top of his skull. He sank to a crouch, propping himself up with one arm. The other tried to raise the machete, subsequently dropping it.

"Stop it!" tried Amanda again.

Wet punches of the hammer continued, over and endlessly over again. Cracks and crunches resounded in splattering cuffs each time the hammer struck him.

After several long minutes, the girl finally stopped. She stood before him, the hammer by her thigh, wearing a wet slicker of his blood, heaving breaths. Her hair was wild and tangled in red knots.

He looked up at her, blood streaming from under the masking, flooding over his eyes, through the ragged holes.

Amanda had never seen so much blood shed from anything. How was he still alive? How could he be moving about on his own merit?

The girl flipped the hammer around, claw-end out, and brought it down. Centered on his forehead, the claw punctured inward and stayed there.

His eyes flickered, sputtered. Then he collapsed onto his side, motionless.

Amanda, revolted and dolorous, looked on. She slowly worked at pulling the knife through her hand, not out. More damage could be done if she retracted it the same way it came in. Thankfully, it was a small blade, with no hilt. She cried out, wincing, tears dotting her eyes. Her skin made a sloppy sound like wet paper as the knife made its way through.

When the effort was done, she held it in the palm of her hand, slimy and murky like a slug.

The girl stood with her back turned to Amanda. Her whole body moved with her heavy breaths. Blood-caked from her hair to her ankles, she gave a look back over her shoulder.

"Are you all right?" asked Amanda.

The girl nodded.

Amanda stood up with a groan. She went and retrieved her gun where it had landed several feet away. She looked back to the girl. "Do you know him?"

The girl shook her head.

"I found…your friends, I guess they were. The authorities are probably there now. There's others combing the woods searching for you, and me too, I imagine."

"Hmm…"

"We need to get back to my car. It's going to take a while to get back there. I don't know any shortcuts this far out."

The girl nodded in response, again.

"Think you can make it?" asked Amanda.

The girl turned around. Her face, breasts, and stomach were smeared and slick in blood. "Can you?"

Amanda shrugged. "I think so."

"I think so, too." She approached Amanda. "But just give me a second."

She staggered to a tree, taking an agonizing seat in front of it. She threw the chain over to the side of her body.

"Can that come off?"

The girl shrugged. "I don't know how."

"I can try and get it off for you."

"Hell…I'm used to it now." She pulled off her shoe. Her white sock was stained red nearly all over.

"My god," Amanda muttered.

"I hadn't noticed how bad my feet were hurting until now." She started to cry.

"The adrenaline kept you from feeling a lot of pain."

Amanda walked over to the girl but stopped when she started tugging at her sock. It took some effort to remove it. When it was finally peeled away from her foot, what was unveiled was a mangled limb of open sores, busted callouses spewing blood and puss.

The girl sniveled even more, dripping wet tears onto her red painted skin. Clear lines cut through the dark tint.

"Wow, that's really bad." Amanda felt stupid for pointing out the obvious to the person who knew exactly how bad it really was. She remembered her backpack tucked away in some brush. "Give me a second to grab something. Will you be okay if I leave you alone for a minute?"

The girl nodded, backhanded her tears. She smeared the blood on her face, making it look like makeup being sweated off.

"Okay, be right back."

Amanda rushed off. She stepped out of the clearing and immediately regretted having done it. She hurried over to the brush where she'd left her pack. For a moment she expected not to find it. Either she'd forgotten where she'd left it, or someone had come along and taken it.

Who?

Anyone. In these woods, Amanda was quickly starting to understand, anything was possible.

The backpack was there. She sighed a relieved breath as she bent down and snatched a strap in her hand. She threw it over her shoulder, then hurried back to the clearing.

Nothing had changed.

The man was in a bloody, ruined heap to her right, and the girl sat on the ground with her foot in her lap, head bent over it. Crying.

"I'm back."

The girl nodded.

Amanda dropped down in front of the girl, stifling back a groan of pain when the backpack struck the wound on her arm. She noticed through the splashed blood on the girl's arms that she had a couple holes on each. She wanted to ask her what happened but didn't want to risk her acknowledging how much they hurt as well. This disgusting foot problem was bad enough on its own.

She let the bag drop between them and opened it. Sifting through the inside, she found the plastic baggy with the first-aid supplies. She yanked it out, then tossed the backpack out of the way.

Amanda showed her the bag. "Not really a doctor-recommended storage case, I'm sure."

The girl smiled. It was nice to see. She held up her shoe. "Not made for constant running I guess."

Amanda frowned. "No, I suppose hiking was about all they were built for."

"These damn things cost almost two hundred dollars. I bought them two weeks ago and wore them to work to break them in."

Amanda noticed how the girl's breasts shook each time she moved. She should probably loan her the shirt tied around her waist. She was hesitant because of the blood, then realized it didn't matter. She doubted she would be wearing it ever again after they fired her later.

Tugging it off her waist, she leaned up, throwing the shirt around the girl's shoulders. "Wear this. You might feel, not as exposed…"

"Thank you." The girl looked at herself. "Oh…I'm getting blood on it…"

"I don't care."

Amanda noticed the hole in her shorts. "I don't have anything for that, though."

The girl looked down, saw the tear, then rubbed the exposed patch of skin with a finger. "Yeah." She sighed. "Can you believe a girl did this to me?"

"Are you serious?" She looked at the man. "I thought it was him."

"No…those hillbillies…"

Amanda remembered the stories, how the farmers liked to take turns on the victims.

"…the sister, Missy. She did this. But you know…she was such a sweet girl. One of those you couldn't help but fall in love with, even if she did do this to me." She looked as if she were about to say more but stopped.

Amanda shushed her. "You can talk about that later. Let's get you bandaged up so we can get moving."

"Oh—okay." She shook her head. "Poor Missy."

Amanda's frown deepened. She was surprised how much remorse the girl felt. Not just that, but guilt. She must have been the one who killed her. No way would she feel that bad if someone else had done it.

She took the tube of antibiotic ointment and squirted some cream onto the palette of sores and went to work. Using cotton swabs, she smeared her foot in ointment. She moved to the narrow slit at the back of her calf and moved up to the chunky crater on her thigh.

"You are one tough cookie," said Amanda. "You know that?"

The girl smiled. "I don't feel like it right now."

"You are." She ripped off a bandage from the small

roll of gauze and applied it to her thigh. "I'm Amanda by the way. Don't know if you remember me."

"I do. I'm Megan."

Amanda almost snapped her finger and shouted: *That's it!*

Megan winced, sucking in a sharp breath.

"Sorry." said Amanda, adding tape to the gauze to hold it in place. Finished there, she wrapped one wrist, then the other.

Megan looked at Amanda's arm. "You're hurt pretty bad, too."

"It's okay. It looks worse than it feels."

"Still, that's pretty bad. Is there going to be enough of this stuff for you?"

Amanda shrugged. "Don't worry about me right now."

"I hope these fuckers didn't have any diseases because if they did, I have them now."

"We both would."

"That would suck for us."

"Sure would."

"That'd be a fitting end to all this, huh? We get out alive and turns out we're dying of AIDS."

Amanda resisted a shiver. She wished Megan wouldn't talk like that. She understood why she was saying it, though. She was scared. Simple as that. Talking it out made her feel better, so Amanda would let her.

Megan continued to ramble on about diseases as Amanda moved on to her foot. She used what was left of the roll mummifying her foot, then grabbed the other roll to finish.

"Thank you for doing that," said Megan.

"You're welcome."

"I see there's some left. Let me wrap your arm."

"It's okay."

"Please. I'm a nurse, okay?"

"You are?" She made a nonbelieving face. "Sure you're not just saying that."

"I'm sure. I work in the ER."

"No shit."

"No shit at all."

"All right, then I'd be honored to have you wrap my arm."

They both laughed, and Amanda assumed Megan was just as clueless as to why. Nothing funny had been said.

"You have hand sanitizer in here?"

"No."

"Damn. Wish there was some way I could rinse out the wound."

"That'd be good, but I don't have any and didn't pass a stream on the way in."

"I can't remember if I've seen any."

"It's okay for now."

"It'll have to do is more like it."

Amanda nodded. "True."

It was Amanda's turn to wince when the cream filled the hole like cement being put into a cavity. Megan squeezed the tube flat, getting out all that was left, which wasn't much.

"What about your other foot?" she asked.

Megan shook her head. "We'll leave it. I'm ready to get out of here but want to make sure you're somewhat taken care of."

"I can't imagine what you've gone through."

Megan stopped a moment. "Yeah." She got back to work, rolling the gauze over her arm like a half-sleeve. She took the tape and stuck the tip to the rest. "I can't even remember what yesterday was like, before all this happened. It seems like I've been stuck in these damn woods all my life."

Amanda smiled. "I know what you mean."

"You're all set."

"Ready to go?"

"*More* than ready."

Amanda stood up, holding out her good arm for Megan.

Megan smiled. "I appreciate the offer, but if you pull on either one of my arms, I might pass out."

Amanda felt like an idiot. "Sorry, I forgot."

"It's okay. I'll manage."

"No, I'll get behind you."

She walked around to the backside of Megan and slid an arm under her. As Megan strained with her legs, Amanda hefted her up. Once she was on her feet, Amanda held the shirt so Megan could slide her arms through. Then, like Megan was her child, she stepped around the front of her and buttoned the shirt up.

Amanda nodded once. "Now we can go."

26

The sun was birthing night, discharging a swath of warm colors across the flattening sky. The last half of their trip through the woods had to be monitored with Amanda's flashlight. They'd stopped only a couple times to sip from the bottle of water in Amanda's bag and nibble on some beef jerky.

She'd done a good job keeping Megan going. Without her support and constant tugging, she would have surely given up fifteen minutes into the hike.

They exited the pitch-black woods to a landscape filtered in orange and red. Only half of the sun remained above the shadowy peaks in the distance. Megan was bowled over by how lovely a sunset it was. In its lovely hues, she saw something in it she had forgotten existed after the day's dealings. Hope. It still existed. The sun was setting on this horrific day, reminding her that tomorrow was all new.

She felt a smile on her dry, brittle lips at the notion.

It was welcomed.

Thank you.

Up ahead, she spotted a Jeep parked on the side of the road like a sanctuary. She tore away from Amanda, crying, walking a few feet on her own before dropping to her knees and leaning forward like someone lost in the desert who just found water.

"We're out! Holy shit we're *out!*"

Amanda laughed. "Yeah, but we're not done just yet."

Megan wanted to kiss the ground. With tongue. She was so happy to be out of the woods that she was giddy. She pulled wisps of grass and let them fall from her fingers.

Amanda came to help her up, but Megan politely declined with a wave of her hand. She stood on her own. She suddenly felt as if she could run all the way home. Her motivation had been rejuvenated. They were going to get away.

Holy shit, they were actually going to make it.

As they walked along, approaching the gravel of the road, Megan noticed a short trail of red dots spattered through the grass. It looked as if it was leading to the road as well. She was about to say something, but Amanda beat her to it.

"I'm going to radio the tower, let them know what's happened. I think they will probably put up a safety point near the station. We can cut down one of the dirt roads and get there around nine."

Megan followed Amanda around the back of the

Jeep to the passenger side where she opened the door up front. Megan opened her mouth to speak, but Amanda had already begun assisting her into the seat. Once both feet were in the floorboard, she quickly said, "Amanda?"

Amanda looked at her. "Yeah?"

She was ready to tell her about the blood in the grass but noticed the look on Amanda's face waver into something concerned and confused.

"What…the hell?"

Megan saw her eyes were focused down by her thighs. She looked down and saw a radio lying in the floorboard. Smashed.

Amanda shook her head. "How…?"

"Who could've done this?"

"Hang on…"

Amanda walked around to the front of the Jeep. "Someone's tampered with the motor."

"How do you know?"

"Wires are hanging out the front of it."

Megan felt a hornet's nest of dread in her stomach. How were they going to get out of here now? She couldn't walk anymore even if she tried. Just moments ago, she'd felt like she could have carried the mountain on her back but that instance of valor was gone. Reality had returned and it brought her pain back with it.

Amanda joined Megan, reaching between her legs. She opened the glove compartment. She dug around inside and came back with a cell phone, then slammed the hatch closed. She checked the screen, and cringed.

"I don't have any bars, but it looks like we're high enough up that I'm getting some kind of signal. I'm going to try and call the tower."

"Do you think you'll get through?"

Amanda didn't acknowledge the question. She handed Megan her gun. "Hold this."

"Amanda."

"I want you to stay in the Jeep. Don't come out unless you have to."

"What are you going to use for a weapon?"

Ignoring the question, she said, "Remember, don't come out unless you have to. Keep the doors locked." She shut the door, then pressed the remote.

Megan jumped at the thumping of the locks.

She watched Amanda step back to the front of the car, holding the phone in the air in search for a stronger signal.

"Well, this beats all, doesn't it?"

Megan looked beside her and found Allison sitting behind the wheel. "Wha...? You?"

"I'm back." She smiled, and there was a staccato of pops in her neck when she turned to Megan. "Miss me?"

"What are you doing here?"

"Well..." She chewed on her lip. "I came to take you with me."

Megan stared blankly at her.

Allison added, "I couldn't go to the other side unless you were with me."

"I don't...what?" The confusion that altered her

face was so strong it hurt. "What are you talking about?"

"See, at first I thought it was you that he wanted, and maybe it was for a while, but then it became clear that it was *her*." She pointed out the windshield. "They had to be brought together, so that's what I did. I led her to him. I tried to get you all together at the hut. Remember the place?"

How could Megan forget? She'd spent time being cozy with a corpse, the insects infesting its rotted flesh trying to invade her own.

"I failed. She wasn't close enough yet. She eventually found the hut but you two had already moved on." Allison shrugged a crackling shoulder. "Can't blame a girl for trying, right?"

Megan couldn't bring herself to react. Her mouth moved, small squeaks escaping, no words.

Allison gave Megan a look like she was about to tell her she was going to be downsized. "I'm sorry, sweetie. But I think you were supposed to die at the camp, too. For some reason, you didn't, and that threw everything out of whack. I believe she was supposed to find *all* our bodies, and that was going to get him and her together. Like yin and yang, you know. Two sides of every coin, etcetera. But it didn't happen like that. And these woods, this mountain? It's wicked land. Haunted. And it gets what it wants. From what I understand that woman is supposed to be his adversary, his final girl. Not you. I believe only she can stop him."

"You're not making any damn sense, Al!"

"It doesn't have to make sense, Meg. Your part's done. My part's *way* past done. And *her* role in all this is just beginning. It's time for him to wrap things up with you so he can go after *her*. Don't worry, it'll be fairly quick, then we can get out of here."

Megan looked through the windshield and could see Amanda cussing at the phone. Several yards ahead of her, a figure emerged from a field of waist-high weeds. This person was cloaked, head hidden underneath the hood-like veneer. An old, withered branch was being used as a walking stick. The jut of a huge hump was on her back. Even from here, Megan could tell the skin was haggard and old, with threads of white hair slung out from the hood.

Megan knew who it was without having to be told. Those ghost stories that had given the Judds many sleepless nights were real.

Missy's voice reverberated through her head, echoic and ethereal: *A witch…a witch…a witch…*

Amanda hadn't seen her.

"She's not going to see her," said Allison, answering the question that hadn't formed in Megan's head. "Just you. I saw her right before I died, too. I had to bring her to you. I couldn't leave until Zeb slayed you. We belong to her now."

The witch woman raised her arm and pointed an arthritis-gnarled finger directly at Megan.

A scream tickled the back of her throat.

Then Megan heard a scuffle of movement behind her. Saw a flash of skin just before a large, beefy hand slapped over her mouth. She could feel the damp wrappings of a provisional bandage on the hand. A bandage that covered a wound she'd caused. The stench of filth and rot wafted up her nostrils. Her screams were muffled behind his hand.

He yanked her head back against the seat. There was a metallic swish, followed by tearing fabric, then came a cold pinch at her back. It became a searing heft as the machete tore its way through her front.

Eyes rolling back in her head, she gargled as blood splashed against his hand, leaking through the cracks of his fingers in tiny rivulets. Her body twitched, jerked. The machete spun this way and that, twisting as she coughed, choking on the blood flooding her lungs.

"All right," said Allison. "Let's go. She's waiting for us."

Megan felt herself being pulled from her body. Below her, she could see the man crouched in the back of the Jeep, holding her by the head with his left hand and using the right to wiggle the machete. Her blood had coated the dashboard and windshield in hot red spatters and splashes.

As a finishing touch, the maniac wrenched her head, snapping her neck in a cracking holler.

27

Amanda heard the click in her ear of the phone call connecting. It rang once, twice, then beeped twice. She looked at the screen and saw *Lost Signal* displayed in the tiny square.

"Dammit!"

If she couldn't reach the tower, that meant they would be walking. She doubted Megan could go much further. And she definitely didn't want to leave her here and hike back without her. With the condition the Jeep was in when they'd gotten here, she wouldn't want to stay by herself either.

Camp.

Maybe that was the best idea. The two of them should set up camp for the night. By morning they will probably have been found by searchers in the woods, or the chopper would be in the sky looking for them. Someone was bound to find them.

They could get a fire going and stay up all night

keeping guard. They had her gun, and if the authorities were doing third shift hunts, they would see the flames. So, staying here and waiting for help was probably the wisest choice.

Amanda hated the idea, but it was all they had.

She heard the click of the Jeep door opening, Megan probably coming to check on the progress. She dreaded telling her they would have to wait here until someone came to rescue them.

Some hero she was. Rescuing Megan only to tell the poor girl they would now *both* need to be rescued.

Turning around, she expected to find Megan limping towards her, using the Jeep as a crutch. Instead, she found no one. Just the door hanging slightly opened, rocking a little from the subtle breeze.

Her eyes panned to the right. Locked on the blood smeared windshield.

Bringing her hand to her mouth, she loosed a shrill gasp. "Megan?"

The door flew open. She heard the hinges gripe as they were pushed back too far in their crevices. The Jeep bounced, swayed, as something big moved around inside.

Amanda took an involuntary step back.

The man arose from the Jeep. His squalid boots slapped the ground one after the other as he stalked his way to the front of the Jeep. No way could he have survived what Megan did to him and yet here he was, drenched in his own blood. Purple welts and gashes covered the exposed areas of his body like giant, bloody measles.

Trying to find her breath, Amanda lowered her hand. The phone slipped from her fingers and fell to the ground.

He lowered the machete down by his side, the hefty blade hanging by his ankle. He leered at her through scowling eyes.

She felt for her gun. Then she remembered she'd let Megan keep it.

It's still in the Jeep!

Amanda took another step back, and he took one more forward. She glanced over her shoulder, seeing nothing but darkening woodland behind her. The last of the golden glow being smothered by a blanket of fog.

Her speed increased with each step back. So did his with each one forward.

Finally, she put her back to him and ran, arms pumping, kicking up dirt behind her. She stole a glance over her shoulder and saw he was now running as well, coming after her.

ABOUT THE AUTHOR

Kristopher Rufty lives in North Carolina with his three children and pets. He's written numerous books, including *Hell Departed*, *Anathema*, *Jagger*, *The Lurkers*, *The Skin Show*, *Pillowface*, and many more. When he's not writing, he's spending time with his kids, or obsessing over gardening and growing food.

He can be found on Facebook and Twitter.

More titles from Kristopher Rufty!

Hell Departed: Pillowface Vs. The Lurkers
Anathema
Master of Pain
(written with Wrath James White)
Something Violent
Seven Buried Hill
Desolation
Bigfoot Beach
The Lurking Season
Jagger
Prank Night
The Skin Show
Proud Parents
Oak Hollow
Pillowface
The Lurkers
Angel Board

Jackpot
(written with Shane McKenzie, Adam Cesare, & David Bernstein)
A Dark Autumn

Collections:
Bone Chimes

Printed in Great Britain
by Amazon